## Praise for Bev Jafek's *The Sacred Beasts*

Pushcart Prize finalist Bev Jafek's The Sacred Beasts is a fiercely feminist novel that makes space for women's stories and art in the midst of macho arenas . . . All the characters are forceful presences in this atmospheric novel that is all about valuing women's ideas, stories, art, and bodies."
— Rebecca Foster, *Foreword Reviews*

"In the eponymous metaphor of sacred beasts, the novel presents an affirmative vision of the potential of LGBT people that is romantic yet subtle, and on several levels, intellectually provocative." — Jim Clark, *GLBT Literature*

## Praise for Bev Jafek's *The Man Who Took a Bite Out of His Wife, and Other Stories*

"Jafek spins tales of grand guignol that soar with unanticipated lushness."
— *The Village Voice*

"Bev Jafek drives a sharp tongue through the conventions of science, marriage and literature. You know you're in the presence of a brainy woman who has taken a look at the world, shuddered and laughed."
— Grace Paley

"Bev Jafek's bustling semi-toxic comedy has a severe intellectual basis, like Ionesco's, and I relish the outrageous confidence of her work." — Paul West

# A
# kind of
# PARADISE

# A
# Kind of
# PARADISE

# Bev Jafek

GusGus Press • Bedazzled Ink Publishing
Fairfield, California

978-1-945805-92-9 paperback

On the cover
Huichol Indian art from the folk art collection of Bev Jafek,
photographed by Elberta Lynn Gaither, 2016.

Cover Design
by

GusGus Press
a division of
Bedazzled Ink Publishing Company
Fairfield, California
http://gusgus.bedazzledink.com

# part one
## the poet

WHEN THE TWO women first saw the tiny Mexican village beneath low, rolling hills, it struck them as a kind of Eden. It was Jean who first used that word, uttered the myth. Words, those unkempt, wayward fountains, oddly ardent bedfellows, were immediate with her. They flowed out of her like some swollen, deep-running river, close to flood. Red, her lover and partner on the trip, would never have used that word. She said nothing, but her normally quick, sly smile was as slow, gentle, and spontaneous as your grandmother's. She was already a Believer. It came not as revelation but a sudden expiration of breath: yes, they had found it, a kind of paradise. They never knew they were looking for it.

They first told me about the village over beer at my favorite lesbian bar, Maud's Study, in San Francisco. Where else would we hold forth so merrily on Eden? Only where the most threadbare dreams and shimmering, sacred mysteries all begin—and end. Who am I to know? I'm Lynne Lonidier, perpetual pundit and diehard local of San Francisco, the crazy lesbian poet on the hill in the Mission, drinking buddy to the most scantily-clad followers of Wicca, rock-hard bitches, foul-mouthed drag queens, poetasters and gourmands, and druggy-fuzzy know-it-alls in this town, the madwoman who lives with a pet dog, cat, snake, fish, rat, and lizard. I'm democratic, if nothing else. A loudmouth in luxury bursts with an extra room in her little house with a hopelessly overgrown garden and seven trees around it like some religious shrine. I'm the woman people tell their stories to, owner of a room that's always open to every sad soul who's had the life and dreams crushed out of her like that blackened, stone-dead cigarette.

It was so unexpected, Jean continued. The fraternal din at Maud's was lower then, and I could almost hear if I tried. I always try. They had picked a town spontaneously on a map, a way they often traveled on their vacations. They craved adventure, the unexpected, and they found it, as life so perversely grins and throws dice. The chosen city in Mexico was roughly central to the jagged country that's shaped like a crumpled, pungent old boot. So they chose it, center of the world, budget bullseye.

At first, they said, it shocked them: the city was amazingly wealthy, not Mexico's image at all, with palatial stone homes covered with ivy and decoratively grilled bars over every entry. That was the first discordant note: those bars everywhere. What were they keeping out, or in? Later, they discovered that their spontaneous vacation pick was none other than the home of Mexico's wealthy upper-class, corrupt bankrollers of the equally corrupt PRI political party that sprouted like a single gorged, nefarious weed from Mexico's revolutionary socialist past, Zapata and his hoard. It was home to the guerrilla opposition; too, terrorists who called themselves Maoists and blew up a local palace from time to time. That was before they killed a few too many tourists from the States. Killing Mexicans was one thing, but dead tourists meant trouble for the wealthy that remained. So, the guerrillas were "taken out," as the kids say today, erased like teacher's chalk on the shrieking blackboard of life's soundless, unknown heart of violence. All things have their intrinsically dependent opposites in the dynamic of history, for I was drunk enough to be a Maoist.

With no interest in these well-guarded palaces, Jean and Red walked to the outskirts of the city over an ancient wooden bridge, just outside its Plutocratic largesse: a small, creaking bridge that might have been dangerous to cross but for the equally small rushing brook just beneath it. Jean instantly loved the sound of it: a rushing, wailing, softly punctuated burst that never ceased; all elements merged and of the same weight; a medium fashioned of multitudes of pebbles hitting jets of flowing water; the soft clanging hum of a monk's chant; a sound singing that all things run together into perfect pitch, harmony, equality; how the universe seems certain moments, precious ones, that vanish with the current.

It was the sound that announced the village's meaning, as the grilled bars had announced the wealth and inequity of the palaces behind them. Over the bridge, they found the tiny Mexican village of their newfound, ancient dream and its music, festival, and people. For it was here The People lived—impoverished, short, stunted, and thin with shining, black-bean eyes and smiles that broke into the manifold resonances of the have-nots that ever had Eden. Some sort of festival was going on, as it always was, with no more reason for being than Eden itself, and a crowd of tiny folk took them by the hand and led them into a ring of dancers. There was a small wooden Ferris wheel that could barely turn, abundant, free-roaming goats, chickens, and donkeys with eyes of soft, reflected light, pooling to small, round lakes of limpid, animal joy.

They were invited to dance with these men, many in wide-brimmed hats, who were all at least a foot shorter than they. They looked about at so many upstart animals, impossibly alive faces, spare men and their women fuller in long, embroidered skirts and deep-necked blouses. Suddenly, a man's voice shouted, "*Mamasotos!*" at which they all shared a burst of laughter like gunshot.

They did not wish to dance like oversized elephants in a ring, but the crowd's laughter was infectious. Yes, so they must be *mamasotos* to this tiny folk. They stood aside, bought thick, creamy Mexican beers from stands, and began to walk about the town, so different from the one across the rickety bridge and that different, again, from the one across the big iron border with the States.

This village was but a few meters from the other town. In the waning sunset and beginning starlight, the magical twilight hour, they saw the diminutive glory of the village. The residents were poor and their houses small; yet, they painted them in rich, saturated hues of deep ochre and umber, earthen, and tended them with scrupulous care. It was not the angry carelessness of poverty in the States. No, each home was a work of joyous folk art: luminously bright, trumpeting its breathtaking detail in latticework, gardens, and woodwork about roofs, doors and windows, with not a single set of bars. It bespoke a reverence for the surface of the world, what one caresses and knows like a lover, nature itself, the everything so easily forgotten.

As they passed from the last street to a profusion of greenery around a lake and the first low, gentle hill that seemed to whisper for its nightfall motion in the slow wind, Jean saw a pair of eyes emerge from the darkness of the last street, not smiling. But she turned her face into the wind and imagined that a donkey or a deer had glanced at them. Red looked more intently, then seeing the eyes vanish, turned full into the sheer power of the windy world. The growing starlight and now the moon were sparkling over the lake, turning it into a sheen of tremulous, first love much like their own; new yet blissfully old, as though we could nearly remember a distant harmony in a past that was our only perfection: Eden. For it must be this low, reachable mountain, a lake, a summer night, a first love, and a tiny town where a festival, ancient and eternal, was taking place. Yes, it was what had been lost in the worlds, for there were many, that they knew. Eden, Jean said it, and it was true, written forever in that place where they dreamed and took breath.

Red, the taller and more boyish, held Jean as they looked over the lake. She was the one to plan things, chop the wood, make the myth true and incontrovertible. She said they would retire here after their many years in those shadowy jungles of San Francisco, some rough and dirty, some soft as a kiss. They could not own land under Mexican law, but they could lease it for decades. Then they would build their house in paradise, the one with three stories, balconies, and many windows without bars, walls of them, overlooking the lake. Yes, Jean said softly, hypnotized.

But I have left out the heart of their story, an easy thing to do, as we sat so easily at Maud's, telling stories on another summer night, with doors and windows nakedly open and inviting, not the usual practice at Maud's. Our Edens are not Biblical: they, too, are older and newer than that rendering of the tale. This particular Eden began in the mid-to-late '60s, when we all arrived in San Francisco for the first time; age of miracles, messiahs on every doorstep, noisy in the streets, lounging in every alleyway. That unspeakably beautiful time when we uttered only oracles and myths, imagining them spanning eternity, and full of flowers, the eternal newly born, flowers and garlands on every self-crowned head, the last time we ever dreamed. Until years, lifetimes later, and the small Mexican village—or Arusha below Kilimanjaro or Belize or Rio or Sri Lanka before the war or wherever it was, for you've told me the story many times. It was a place and you found it; the flower still moist behind your ear, the earring dangling beneath it. Now you must return, if you still can: you're marked. And if you don't, you are old and finished by that fiendishly precise measure. Back in the '60s when the fountain first rose up, even I—the foul, mad, old hoary one, covered with my bristles and brambles and poetry—had nought but flowers falling from my lips and pen, my beer mugs overflowing, my house on the hill growing from a tender vine.

More fortunate than most, they stayed together all those years, avoiding all the fateful-faithless traps and lusty, glowing quicksand, growing rumpled into one another—knotted and tree-like—as women do. They saved their money; it was natural to them, unlike the bolder dreamers. They were both librarians: they even worked together and had first met in the library. San Francisco's public library, as none other, could be such a gentle bud of lesbian love. They were not impressive wage earners nor were they wealthy, but it was enough, saved scrupulously, for just one dream—at least at Mexican prices.

I remember—it was but a year ago, 1993—when they packed their few and frugal things and set out for Mexico, the final leg of the journey that still hovered, airborne, in a dream. Red was portly then and had high blood pressure; Jean was still girlishly slim with low blood pressure. Both had leonine manes of thick, white hair that still glowed in the sun. Red had flown to Mexico earlier and negotiated a contract for several acres of property overlooking the lake, just as they had planned. They worked through a Mexican lawyer, and the resulting lease gave them four decades. The lawyer also negotiated a contract with a builder using local workers, children of the throng who had once greeted them on that fateful night so long ago. They had arranged a residence for three months, after which they thought it possible to live in a portion of the house to be; though it would take a few more months to fully construct it.

That was in the spring of 1993. As I bid them goodbye, I thought, as I often do, of all the dreamers who had not come so far. Perhaps a dreamer needs something of a librarian's patience and equilibrium to triumph and fly off, still imbued with youthful light, in the bright, cold, harsh sunlight of San Francisco, light reflected from white and pastel buildings, so unflattering to dreamers as they age. I envied them and inevitably, I feared for them and even prayed in my odd poet's fashion, my own perversely intractable chant of awe and readiness for revelation that vanishes with the next day's bitter grains of espresso.

Then I rarely heard from them and distantly—postcards, letters when we felt nostalgic for the past, some exuberant phone calls on holidays. This is what I know: they first spent a long time swimming in that lake. What better sport for Eden? Again, they struck the town with wonder as the giant amphibious, white-haired old ladies from America disported themselves like young otters in the softer Mexican sun. At night, they strolled about the town, as they had so long ago. Many of the exquisite folk art dwellings remained and had vastly grown in number, though the town was still as poor. They rarely went over the bridge to see the stone palaces, which were just as carefully guarded as long ago. There were now many more people living in shantytowns further away from the lake, and the beautiful, tiny dwellings now housed a small Mexican middle-class. When they strolled too far and encountered the shantytowns, far more numerous, they felt distressed to find the residents as poor, thin, and dirty as those anywhere in the third world, Bombay to Lima.

Then they began the long task of supervising the builders as well as swimming in the lake. These men, as thin and small as those so long ago, took orders well in Spanish and initially, the architect was present. Though the two women were fluent in Spanish, they could not understand all of the endless exclamations and badinage of the builders. The men appeared to speak frequently in an unknown slang mixed, possibly, with an ancient tonal language spoken in the Yucatan. The architect yelled at them frequently in the same argot, and they felt a tension building that remained a mystery to them. By the end of the day and the long, umber shadows of evening, still a magical time, all tensions had dissipated in fatigue, and the men smiled broadly and went home to their unknown lives. The two women liked to imagine them dwelling in the tiny, exquisite homes that ringed the lake; but often, they suspected many were shanty-town dwellers, particularly the very thin ones who came to work late and were often disheveled, drunk, or both, as though they might have slept in an alleyway. Poverty as they knew it in the States had filtered soundlessly across the border in the long, intervening years. At times, they admitted that the town was no longer an Eden and could never have been. They began serving a large, nutritious lunch daily to the men and inquired of various civic groups whether they could do anything to alleviate the town's poverty and inequity of wealth. When this drew a blank, costing vastly more than they would ever have, they behaved like good librarians and donated a large Spanish collection of books to a free, public library. They remained, in other words, true to their dream and indeed, it took strength and loyalty to persevere.

This I sensed from our contacts, though they had not returned to San Francisco. The house with a second story of windows without bars grew in stature, and they were able to live in the interior and lock the door at night. They moved most of their possessions in and began to feel content.

One late afternoon, Jean's eyes at last passed over the entire beloved interior of their former home in San Francisco. She had spent most of the day gardening, and she wanted to bathe and rest. Yet, for a moment she lingered over the sight of the bright drapes from Guatemala, the rugs from Peru, and the paintings of the desert from a brilliant Southwestern Indian artist they had once met in Taos, a miserable alcoholic who painted landscapes bathed in clouds of shimmering, cosmic light, a man who seemed to see heaven and earth at once and live unable to reconcile them. She could still see his deeply lined, craggy face, vastly older than its years.

It was all here now: the Berber chairs and couches, the desks and tables in perfect wood that nearly resembled flesh, the handiwork, again, of Indian artisans. If the town was no longer Eden, the lake was, she decided, and so was the house. It was enough: that elusive state never quite what one expected but ever sufficient for life and that bit of integrity without which no dreams survive. She opened the desk drawers, noting as she had so many times, that they moved as things made of velvet, inconceivably fine workmanship. Lying in one drawer was a loaded revolver, Red's inevitable addition to the house. Even the gun glowed softly in the sunset, for Jean had not pulled the drapes yet. The gun was an unlikely addition to Eden and, with an equally unlikely response; she smiled, then laughed.

She was remembering the only time it had ever been fired. I had heard the story at least twice in our long, rambling evenings at Maud's. It happened many years ago, when they bought their first house together in the hinterlands beyond San Francisco, rural and rustic towns north of Berkeley that were known to be red of neck and Republican. Jean gardened scrupulously and had created a strip of lawn with many-hued roses on rocky, unproductive soil. Then a mole came to dwell beneath them and the roses withered. At night, he dug his subterranean caverns with hairless paws and fed upon their tender roots, growing fat and careless. Jean and Red often discussed their vexation with this mole. The roses seemed innocence debased, then womanhood most vulnerable, then they saw mole blood.

In fury, one day Jean took the gun outside with her and flooded the mole's network of caverns with a garden hose. She intended to either drown it or shoot it if it came up for air. As water coursed into the first and then the whole cavernous network, she anxiously called to Red. The hose foamed into the caverns, the minutes passed like eons, and she nervously wondered where on earth the mole was and if it could possibly have escaped. After long, breathless moments, its hideous baldhead at last rose up like a nightmare—pink, drenched, and gasping for air—from the one hole that met the surface. As Jean pointed the revolver, she was suddenly almost in shock at the horror of the mole's ugly pinkish baldness and the dreadful wormlike slenderness of its body: it gaped for breath, its bulbous, blind eyes without irises or pupils in the rare sunlight, its paws upraised to grasp the surface, almost in an attitude of prayer—begging, it seemed, for life—though it could not possibly have seen her. She had never seen a more revolting creature in her life, yet she realized in alarm that she had never killed an animal beyond an insect before. A moment could not be lost since the mole could now breathe; yet, she was engulfed in a flood of conflicting emotions. With its hideous, gaping mouth; blunt, pink snout; bug-eyed sightless stare and imprecating paws; could there be a more despicable thing in the world, yet a more understandable motive than begging for life? Then she felt a firmer, stronger hand cover hers, the gun discharged, the mole—a bloody, pinkish roar—dropped dead into its hole. She looked up into Red's face and realized that her lover had shot the gun for her, killing the mole. She laughed hysterically into Red's shoulder and then said, "Thank you. I couldn't."

Arm in arm, they took a long, deep breath, laughed, and went back into the house, praising the roses that would now have their many-hued birth, oblivious to all else. They had but a half-hour of Eden, for that was the time it took for the police to arrive.

A squat, overfed police officer, ugly as a mole, appeared suddenly on their doorstep, demanding an explanation for the gunshot, which a neighbor had reported. They explained it was but a mole that had been killed and showed the officer the hole, the hose, the withered roses. The officer thanked them and left but, incredibly, returned to the reporting neighbor's home for corroboration. The residence was home to a family that disliked having lesbians for neighbors and was even incensed that the two women argued less than any family on the block. In another half-hour, the plump policeman returned, now full of dark suspicions concerning a couple of perverts, the lesbian Bonnie and Clyde, perhaps, of Molesville. He demanded, somewhat angrily, to see the mole's body. Red's face was now as red as her hair and she said, just as angrily, that the mole had fallen back into its hole and she hoped it would stay there. The policeman, now just as red, demanded that they produce the mole in question. Red marched into the garage, then handed him, furiously, a shovel. Chivalrous at last but just as determined to discover the perverse secrets of lesbian lives, the policeman turned even redder, sweated like a horse, and dug. A portion of the mole's network was unearthed, then another, and still another. "My God, he's going to kill the roses over this," Red whispered with ragged breath. At last, just before the roses were destroyed once and for all, the bloody, filthy, pink little body lay before them like an abhorrent giant worm.

"Well, you got your mole!" Red said sarcastically.

And to their continuing amazement, the officer picked up the tiny, dreadful thing in a handkerchief, deposited it in a plastic bag and carefully sealed it. "This is going to ballistics!" he said triumphantly and swaggered off. Jean drew Red, who was now purple, into the house.

"My darling," she said with careful irony, "we will be vindicated—or at least rid of a dead mole." At last, the two women laughed, and Red's coloring returned to normal.

In three hours, however, another policeman knocked on their door. Much younger and slimmer, the officer gave Red a disarming smile and handed her the mole with but a word of explanation, "Regulations."

"Oh, regulations!" shouted Red, turning red again.

"We must return the remains," he added. To her utter disgust, Red saw that the mole had been refrigerated for possible trial use before a cooler head had prevailed. Now its tiny, pink appendages stuck straight out from its sides, making it all the more loathsome. She hurled the mole over the officer's shoulder and into the street, then uttered a string of classical Greek exclamations and curses from *The Iliad*. "That was unnecessary, ma'am," the officer said curtly. Red slammed the door shut, unnecessarily, and thus the Day of the Dead Mole passed.

The sun had set when Jean, at least three decades later, closed the drawer with a smile. She was very glad, she reflected, that Red was now taking medication for her high blood pressure.

THE HOUSE CONTINUED to grow in its unique largesse, its gift to a world that could not see it for what it was—a pure distillation of will, strength, imagination, and love—to make a thing new to the world, honed by a dream. And, there was always time, the time for the house to take root and form, and time became old to them, an ancient holiday. With such simple elements as heat, sun, afternoon swims, and evening strolls, it was the time of a truth perpetually unfolding, of life, turning circular as time had always been to the Indians themselves.

Sometimes they took short trips to other parts of Mexico. They hired two local women recommended by the architect, Rosa and Blanca, middle-aged matrons with faces lined and grim but sudden in their laughter and the gleam of their black eyes. Rosa and Blanca lived in their home and directed the men as well as making the daily feast. The four women became close to one another effortlessly; Rosa and Blanca seemed to love their time spent in this way for reasons Jean and Red did not fathom, though they speculated with a laugh that their new friends might be lesbians. Whatever the cause, the house was clearly a refuge to Rosa and Blanca. It took time, too, for them all to notice that the men resented being directed by two women from their community, though it was softened somewhat by the feast at noon.

One afternoon, Red and Jean were strolling through the town together with a shopping cart and came upon a bakery full of women. To their delight, the women were talking together with great animation while working. They entered the bakery, intending to buy loaves of bread and pastry. Suddenly they noticed that many of the women had large bruises around their eyes and mouths. They could even see bruises on several women who were turned away from them, marks of belts or whips across their backs. One woman had abrasions around her neck that suggested an attempt at strangulation. To their surprise, the injured women seemed oblivious to these marks and talked with the same spontaneity as the others. They were not ashamed and made no effort to cover their marks, as though bruises were part of the same life cycle as anything else. As they boxed the pastries and loaves of bread, the women smiled broadly and their eyes glowed in their darkness like those of gentle, slow-moving animals.

At that moment, an old man entered from the rear. "No more talk," he yelled. "Get back to work!" Jean and Red were shocked, since the women had been working well, obviously energized by their intimacy. The man's hair was limp and black, his face oily, enflamed, and pocked by some internal degeneration, making him look older than he was. And, he was very drunk. They quickly paid for the bread and pastries, loaded their cart, and left. They looked back to see the man's face twist and distort like a primitive mask as he sized them up, so enraged that he looked scarcely human. Jean thought of the gnarled base of an oak with black eyes leering out.

Outside, they were silent and immediately began to walk home. "That was awful," Jean finally said. "Does he beat them? Is that what it means?"

"More likely their husbands beat them," Red said. "They can get another job, but they're stuck with that husband."

"And that strange man. He hated us, even though we bought his goods."

"We're women with some power and money. He can't control us, so he just vents on the women he employs."

"That's why Rosa and Blanca love staying at our house!" Jean said. "Their children have grown up, and they're alone with their husbands. It's a night free of abuse." Their pain and dismay dangled in the air, tossed about by the playful wind, and the light and heat only pressed against it, that soft chimera of beauty that always touched them, slowed time down. Then, like all builders of a dream, their pain lessened and began to pass away. The very light and dust commanded them to resist, and all they had to do it with was love. They held hands and returned home.

Toward evening, inexplicably, they rose and went outside for another walk. This time, they passed the lake, the colorful houses, the town, and walked directly into the warren of shantytowns. They were silent, guided by instinct; a question hovered over their lives. The shantytowns were much like those they had seen throughout the third-world, lively in their ways of crushing life, hovels made of any material—cardboard, metal, sticks, plastic, even mattresses and cast-offs from garbage. A trench had been dug in back of the hovels for sewage, making it flow slowly downward to another place, anywhere but the town. When Jean and Red looked closely, they could discern a few businesses, bars full of men on makeshift chairs, bathed in a colored light, a bit of fiesta with no celebration or relief. They saw women working together, talking as they washed clothes and tended their children.

They even came upon a Catholic school for the children, but it was empty, dark, long abandoned, settling into dust like the rest of the shantytown. Then cooking odors were everywhere, outdoor fires mixed with smells of the sewers, life and death mixed pungently together as in a jungle. A bit of livestock was being raised, and animals got loose from time to time, children laughing and running after them in a throng. The children were dirty and thin, but often exultant in their play, the love of their mothers, and in the newness of the world, however full of want and filth. The women talked and worked as the men hid in those dark pools of the mind, filled with alcohol, drugs, and hypnotic light, places that were home only to death. Sometimes the women still smiled and laughed, reconciled to pain.

Underneath it all was sound present by day or night, as though walls had never existed, loud and soft, up and down its own crude scales, as omnipresent as a river flowing by—animals yelping and squawking, children shrieking in joy or horror, men and women talking, yelling, screaming. As the two women adapted to it, they could begin to pick out individual groups, couples, men and women together, the men often shouting as women screamed. As they passed one remnant of a hovel still inhabited, they saw a man beating his wife. The woman saw them pass and gaped in awe, as though another universe had suddenly appeared; the man whirled around and bellowed, shaking clenched, hairy fists at them.

Silently, they now walked away from the maze of shantytowns. The question no longer hovered over them. Red had a prickling sensation of something behind her. She looked over her shoulder and saw a figure wearing a devil mask in the dark at the edge of the shantytown. It was red and black with huge, glistening horns, a mustache, and beard, immense eyes with pupils distilled to a point of emotion supernatural in its intensity, and a wide, gaping mouth full of fangs that seemed to be laughing. Inexplicably, Red quickly looked forward again as though she had seen something shameful. She did not understand her alarm and said nothing to Jean.

Just before they reached home, Red asked, "Are you OK?"

"I'm still all right, I guess," Jean said in a tired voice. "Who knows? Maybe we can do something good for them. I wonder how many victims of domestic abuse could live here."

They wanted to talk, about that and only that, but it seemed immense and alien. It was late, too, and they had dinner instead, talked of other things. They read for a short time and then lay down together in the bed that still meant peace, rest, acceptance of what could not be changed. Their love was slow and full of tenderness that night. They held one another for a long time after.

The next day, the men working on the house seemed to be engaged in a bitter argument, and there was complete silence at the noon feast, which was even more unusual. Jean found Rosa and Blanca whispering together on the stairs in the late afternoon. When she asked them what they were talking about, both women were tense and silent, averting their eyes.

"What's this?" Jean asked with a smile. "You know you can tell me anything. Is it something at home? If you need to leave for a time, you certainly can."

"Oh no!" said Rosa in shock. "We want to stay!"

"We *must* stay," Blanca said in a low voice filled with fear.

"Well you know you're always welcome. But what has happened?"

"We don't know for sure. It is just a rumor. It might not have happened again."

"Again?" said Jean. "But *what* has happened again?"

"We shouldn't tell you," Blanca said with pleading eyes. "It does not involve you. You are safe. You will always be safe. Only the others . . ." She looked even more frightened of revealing more.

"Safe from what?" Jean asked, now scrutinizing them carefully. "You're terrified. What is happening here?"

"Don't make us tell you," Rosa said and looked even more distressed. Tears were forming in her eyes.

"All right," Jean said, anxious to calm them. "I won't. You certainly don't have to tell me everything you know. I won't pry. But I hope you know that we will help you if you're in any kind of trouble."

The two Mexican women looked more relieved that Jean would not insist on the truth than that she had offered them her protection. They quickly left, which disturbed Jean even more. Later, she saw them quietly working on the second floor, cleaning the wall of windows. Blanca looked grimly determined and Rosa's eyes had tears.

In the evening, Red and Jean ate their dinner quietly, each wondering what to say to the other. "It was a very strange day," Red began.

Jean expelled a breath of relief. "Wasn't it? I don't know where to begin."

"Oh, you've heard it, too?"

"Only that there's some kind of rumor going around. I couldn't get it out of Rosa and Blanca. They were upset enough for tears."

"I overheard it from the workmen. One man said that a woman had been murdered last night somewhere in the area, then another said it couldn't be happening again and sounded angry. They began arguing and some others joined in. It was clearly something they wanted no repetition of. That's all I could make out. They seemed to be trying to stop us from finding out."

Jean was silent in shock. "I had no idea it was something like a murder. Why didn't they tell me? What were they afraid of?"

Red was silent, looking at Jean in distress. "Well, remember it may or may not be true," she finally said. "Not even the people who've lived here all their lives seem to know for sure. There's nothing about it in the Spanish newspapers."

"Well, then . . ." Jean said and felt a bit relieved.

"And I've been thinking maybe we should get away for a while, go to Ensenada and swim in the ocean for a few days."

"The Pacific!" Jean said in astonishment. "I just realized how much I've missed it." She smiled at Red in gratitude and love. "Oh, yes, let's go, darling. I'm so glad you thought of it. We'll leave the house to Rosa and Blanca. They feel safe here."

And I'll show them where the gun and bullets are, Red thought, but said no more.


THE OCEAN WAS a softly warm, blue-green scarf carrying Jean as she floated on her back, thinking that only the slightest motion of her legs and feet was necessary to stay alive. I have the life of a giant sea turtle that can live for centuries, she thought. The universe is my body barely in movement, a body shaped for eternity. Red was out much further, challenging the big waves. How long have I been like this? Jean wondered. Maybe hours . . . Overhead the first thunderclouds were forming. Jean smiled at them, too. I love it all, she thought, then returned to a standing position with her head barely above water, watching for her lover. Red was now swimming toward her.

Reaching her, Red said, "A downpour can occur very fast in the tropics. We should go back to the shore."

"No, I want to stay for a few minutes and see it come as though I were lying on a lawn looking at the sky. Float with me." Red grinned and began to float just beside her. There was sudden thunder, darkness, and rain. I love this too, Jean thought. If we can just float aimlessly in the universe, we will know everything, the wisdom of a sea turtle. A jagged streak of lightning shot across the sky and a boom of thunder resounded. They could not even hear it with water covering their ears, but experienced it as a choppy wave.

Red pulled Jean up and said, "That's it" with the same broad smile. "We can draw that all that beautiful, nasty stuff toward us." They walked to the shore and then back to their hotel in pouring rain. It was brief.

"I'm ravenous." Jean said. "I had a mystical experience out there."

Red laughed. "That's what vacations are for. And floating in the elements is the preferred way."

After they had washed and were on the street again, Jean bought a Tree of Life sculpture from an old Indian woman sitting on the pavement with her wares in a blanket.

"Now our living room will look like every other Mexican house," Red said. "They sell those things on every street corner."

"Our house *is* Mexican now," Jean said. "I also had a mystical experience when I was a child, seeing one of these sculptures. I had no idea that there were countries and that it was from another one. The tree was everything moving together in concert. That tree was alive and it did not end."

"That's what childhood is for."

They appreciated being in a city again and found a restaurant quickly. Then they were having dinner with wine and feeling more relaxed than they had since leaving the States.

"It is good to be a child of the universe again. That has been lacking for some time," Jean said.

"That's what wine is for."

"Stop that; you're annoying me. You could say, that's what Mexico is for or even, that's what sex is for."

"I was going to say, that's what California is for," Red said, and they laughed.

"It's surprising how stressful building a dream house turned out to be. Could that have been true about a murdered woman?" It seemed very far away from them.

"Well, since they think it happened before, maybe it's just a superstition or a bit of folklore."

"They were really afraid, though."

"Your head can do that easily enough." For Red, it now seemed the moment to tell what she had concealed. "I saw someone in a mask the night before, just outside the shantytowns."

"Following us?"

"No, just there, a distance away."

"What kind of mask?"

"A diablo. They have lots of fiestas, where they dance with masks. The devil is a character in nearly all of them. The Day of the Dead is coming up soon. It's their major holiday, more important than Holy Week though it lasts only two days."

"Is it ominous? Is the mask related in some way? It's a devil."

"Down here, the devil is also a figure of fun and laughter, like Death masks and dancing skeletons on the Day of the Dead. There is no absolute good and evil, heaven or hell or even a real afterlife, in spite of the Catholic influence. They adapt Catholicism to the old Indian religions. We'll see that during the Day of the Dead fiesta. It's a family holiday to honor the dead. There are three deaths to an Indian—physical death, placement in the grave, and then the time when he is finally forgotten by later generations of the living. That's why they create very involved altars with photos of the dead and picnic in the cemeteries with the dead person's favorite foods."

They were silent, and a deep pulse of feeling passed between them. "That is true," Jean said, smiling. "The Indian culture has so much sanity and wisdom to it. The priests are irrelevant. That's why it always seems so much more hedonistic than our culture. It's a good thing we're here." The strangeness of what had happened was gone.


WHEN THEY RETURNED to their house, they found that three more women were living in it, another matron and her two adolescent daughters, all sleeping on the floors, though everything was clean and tidy. "They were so frightened," Rosa said with pleading eyes.

"Of course they can stay here," Jean said, dismissing the issue. *I'd rather have them here than covered with bruises in some bakery,* she thought.

When they were alone again, Red said, "This house is growing more complicated by the day. Maybe we should have built a stupa or a pyramid to live in instead." They laughed.

"Well, that *is* life. It began with a dream and that gives it a uniquely human dignity; let's not forget."

The personalities of the women and girls sheltered in the house soon manifested themselves, and Rosa and Blanca began to acquire a depth and spontaneity they had not shown before. The new mother's name was Josefina, a more assertive and ambitious woman who owned a small café in the town. She was very tall and wore her dark hair short, unlike Rosa and Blanca, whose hair was long and traditionally plaited. Her eyes were brown, empathetic and typically Mexican but for a glint of impatient intelligence like a piece of schist; a sparkling, shifting light characteristic of those accustomed both to giving orders and negotiating in subtle and dangerous situations. Josefina's daughters, Teresa and Clara, were introduced as very good students and seemed to have adopted their mother's assertiveness and self-confidence. Fascinated and curious, Red asked them what work they wanted to do as adults.

Teresa, a tall, strikingly beautiful girl with long, dark hair and translucent, nut-brown skin, answered, "I will be a doctor in a Mexico City hospital." She added proudly, "I was there once."

Clara, two years younger with lighter skin and hair, announced, "I will be a bullfighter. But, I love animals and though I will bravely wave the cape before the bull, I will never kill him. I will not let the picadores hurt him, either. At the end of my performance, when he is tired and defeated and lies down, I will pet him. That will be the end of the show. If no one wants to come and see me do that—well, then I will be a wetback. I will swim the Rio Grande to and from the great *El Norte* no matter what happens." These two answers, so swift, serious and unexpected, caused Red and Jean to laugh, which resulted in surprise and consternation on the two girls' faces.

Teresa asked, "So you don't think we can do it?" with battle on her lovely dark face.

"Oh no," said Red, "we *know* you will and we applaud your ambitions with pleasure."

Clara said imperiously, "So why aren't you clapping?"

Red and Jean clapped and were joined by the other others, who were now laughing, too. Rosa's daughter, Nieves, a small, shy girl with huge black eyes that brimmed with misery, then said very softly, "I will marry and have children."

"Not for *me*," Teresa said.

"I don't have to do that!" exclaimed Clara. "I can beat up any boy my age in school." A fierce gleam showed in the sisters' eyes;

and once again, all the women laughed. Teresa and Clara looked displeased, and Nieves looked even more unhappy.

"Adults are weird and boring," Clara said. "Let's go play." The three girls quickly vanished.

"They're just wonderful," Jean said after they stopped laughing. "They really are." Josefina's eyes shone intently; she clearly loved her daughters in all their eccentricities and believed that they lived in a world that should be challenged.


A PATTERN SOON emerged in their evenings. Josefina worked late at the café, and Rosa and Blanca worked throughout the evening while talking together. Rosa was a seamstress and Blanca, an artist. They brought their materials from home and seemed to be happy and industrious for exceptionally long hours while Teresa and Clara either studied or played together, often with Nieves.

"Quite a house this is becoming," Red said to Jean one night when they were alone.

"It always surprises me, even in its patterns," Jean said.

"How long do you think they'll stay?"

"Not long, I'd guess. Rosa and Blanca will be here often until the house is finished. But, they all seem to have very active lives and will want their own space again. This seems to be a working holiday with the *gringas*, which must be even more surprising to them." The atmosphere was so pleasant that Red and Jean nearly failed to notice that the increase in women being sheltered there disturbed the workmen. Their camaraderie was dampened and their faces were often rigid with anger.

As the Day of the Dead approached, the whole area, palaces to shantytowns, became a fiesta of color, candle-light, and nights that eerily did not seem to end. Rosa and Blanca asked if they could bring their *ofrendas*, or altars for the dead, during the holiday. When Jean and Red agreed, several complex works of folk art suddenly appeared in their living room. The largest and most convoluted, Blanca's, was as big as a small Christmas tree. It had over two dozen photos of the dead and so many flowers, baskets and individuals pieces of art that it seemed to be a folk art museum.

Shaking her head in awe, Red said, "How on earth is this a cult of the ancestors? It looks more like an explosion in a toy store."

"I've never seen anything like it," Jean said. The altar held miniature textiles, decorated plates of clay or enamel, candle-holders with lit candles, colorful clay crosses, skulls, guitars, necklaces, framed paintings, brides and grooms, masked dancers, cars, skateboards, lizards, butterflies, coins, blankets, priests, cats, dogs, devils, angels, cooking utensils, gloves, hats, imaginary beasts, and even a camera.

"How many generations?" Red asked Blanca, wondering how long this scroll of living memory could extend.

"There are others here, too, not my family, women who may not have anyone to mourn and remember them. I add more art to it every year." Immediately, Red and Jean noticed that there were more photos of women than men as well as many young girls.

In a flash of intuition, Jean asked, "Are some of them the murdered women and girls?"

The room was silent. Rosa and Blanca looked up at Jean with faces of shock and fear. Red felt her face flush and that prickling sensation return, though this time she did not turn away from it. "Yes, some of them," Blanca finally said, and the Mexican women continued working in silence.

"Will someone *please* tell me what is going on here?" Red said; and, as their silence continued, Jean and Red reluctantly left the room.

THE NIGHT BEFORE the two-day holiday, Red and Jean returned home in the early evening to find the house full of music and the three girls dancing barefoot on the lawn in elaborately layered, beribboned, and laced floor-length dresses of vivid hues, their faces painted white with black around their eyes, noses and teeth, like skulls. Candles glowed on the grass beside them, and the three swayed slowly and gracefully with great solemnity, twirling their skirts like capes.

"We're practicing for tomorrow," Nieves said.

"Aren't we scary!" Clara shouted.

Inside the house, the living room was filled with skulls made of clay and papier-mâché, all painted in hallucinatory colors and covered with the intricate detail of flowers, animals, suns, planets and what perhaps can only be called explosions. One was bright pink and draped with glimmering spider webs and flowers about the forehead and eyes, a wild-eyed lizard dangling down its cheek. Another was completely covered with squiggles and archetypal signs in all colors, its eyes a vortex, its multi-colored teeth seeming to chatter and dance at once. On other skulls, the eye sockets and noses were decorated with jewelry, animals, spirals, and leaves. One even had smaller skulls in its eyes; others had eyes of lace, beads, crosses, whirlpools, even beer bottles.

"The Day of the Dead will be nothing compared to this," Red said.

She was instantly defied. "No!" shouted the mothers, smiling. "The whole town is doing this!"

"Then who will buy it?" Jean asked.

"Everyone!" was shouted with laughter.

"I have made so many and still they want more," Blanca said. "The Day of the Dead is my best holiday for business."

The concept of business enterprise seemed, to Red and Jean, incongruous in such a riot of color and form. The girls had come inside. Nieves was suddenly confidant and said, "The dead are everywhere and they want to play with us. Everyone wants to play with them." Then Rosa came out of the kitchen with a tray of multi-colored sugar skulls that were offered to all.

"I bow to the inevitable," Red said, and she and Jean put away their groceries and returned to the living room to eat candy skulls. The girls proudly showed them how the group had spent its mornings and afternoons creating *calaveras*, skeletons alone or in scenes. One framed scene showed a skeleton beauty parlor with the skeleton of a woman, legs crossed, in a dress under a dryer talking avidly with another skeleton in a dress, whose sparse hair was being styled by a skeleton hair-dresser. Similarly, there were framed scenes of skeleton robbers and policemen in a bank run by skeletons; skeleton brides in long white dresses with lacy trains and their skeleton grooms in tuxedos; skeleton cowboys riding with herds of skeleton cows across a plain; a skeleton family in a living room, including a skeleton pet dog and a crying baby skeleton in a crib. There were skeleton doctors and patients in an office, skeleton matadors waving capes before skeleton bulls, skeleton priests with their skeleton congregations, and individual frames of skeleton pet dogs, cats and horses, all waving goodbye to their owners. A colossal skull as big as a human torso, to be used as a mask covering the entire head, lay in a corner of the room.

Sampling a sugar skull, Jean said, "I have never been so struck by the brevity of life."

"I have never seen death as so alive," Red said, swallowing the last of a small pink skull.

It's the house, Jean thought. At that moment, she could still see a dark red sunset and layers of sable clouds curling lazily in the sky. The house itself seemed to be a spirit with a will of its own, something rushing in its dark corners, fire just behind its light.

"This calls for wine and a celebration," Red said. "Can you stop working now or do you need the whole evening?"

"Oh, we can always stop work," Blanca said and smiled. The Mexican women looked at one another with a natural Indian understanding that always seemed ready for a fiesta. There it is again, Jean thought, that difference.

They all sat, eating sugar skulls and then drinking wine, commenting on their creations and enjoying the music. "We can show you some of our ancient dances," Josefina said. "We put on masks and costumes and dance our oldest and truest stories. I dance with the *viejas* and *viejos*. I'm not so old, but I like to feel what the end of my life will be like."

Everyone went outside onto the moonlit grass. The three Mexican women danced in a procession while their daughters returned to their solemn twirling of skirts. "I dance with the *tigres*," said Rosa. "It is our most powerful animal spirit."

"When I grow up, I will dance with the tigers, too," shouted Clara in joy. "I want to pounce and have a tail!"

"Oh, I want to dance with the devils," Teresa said. "They have the most fun and they get to be silly, too."

"I like to dance as the lusty woman," said Blanca. "It is so unlike me, and I like to lose myself."

Nieves was silent and looked unhappy again, but Clara only shouted, "What will you dance as?"

"There's not much left," said Nieves.

"Yes, there is, but come with me and dance with the tigers," Clara said. "You get to have claws and a tail and pounce all over people and things."

Nieves began to smile. "If you're there, maybe I can do it. I do want to have a tail, claws and whiskers. I love their whiskers and soft, furry ears."

"I will pet you," Teresa said and the girls laughed.

With such words, the three Mexican women broke into some of the strangest dancing the two American women had ever seen. Red and Jean decided to dance in free-form American fashion since it was all they knew, and then all were barefoot in the grass, dancing under the moon. This is what I'll remember, Red thought. The way it wavered and then came back to paradise.

Or, that's what I imagine she thought, and my guide is the illustrious pit of my stomach. So, you might very well ask, how do I know so much about them, a poet in San Francisco, allowing the images to just flow from her mind and ink from her pen? I know Mexico like an old friend with whom I've shared too many beers, much love and many harsh words. My gods are as old as anyone's, and it is a poet's business to know. But more, I feel the sorrow of the gods looking down on human life, for gods and poets must always grieve as they feel that vivid but frail life twitching along to its close. Yes, I do know the end, and I'm writing the story for Red and Jean, who had the courage to build a dream, to fail and ask for redemption, as we always do, the one that comes from poetry and not the gods, the true one.

So, I know the Day of the Dead began with that soft Mexican sun lightly touching some of the country's most colorful creatures, who in turn were telling its oldest stories to please their own gods. The dancing processions of the fiesta had begun before Red and Jean awoke. It was late morning before they joined the crowds in the street, which were costumed as breathing, walking monuments to Death. They saw the stock characters that the Mexican women had shown them the night before—tigers, devils, old men and women, handsome and young men and women, Christ and many other costumed figures they could not place, though they obviously were characters from a sacred tale, and Death—death in the most various, turbulent and intense forms of life.

Death blew a trumpet in the tiger that had a headdress as large and elaborate as those of the Incas, an ochre and spotted bewhiskered feline face, with devil horns and hair falling inconceivably into multi-colored spheres. Out of the tiger's mouth came a death skull of bright lapis covered with textile-like patterns. Death shouted in a superman costumed with red wings and a cape, a tight-fitting green suit and a huge purple skull covering the dancer's entire head. Death whispered in the airy costumes of skeleton pirates with huge hats full of billowing flowers and flared shirts and pants with satin sashes. All this was done to tease Death, ornament it, steal away its sting.

Red and Jean first plunged into the crowds and then stood on the sidelines, watching the dancers and processions pass. "I don't know how to describe it. I've never known Death to dance a jig, cry out, try to out drink the whole town, parade itself to death, or is it to life?" Red said. "But that's what Death seems to be doing today."

"I've never thought of it as meandering and expanding everywhere, a universe. What can I ever say to describe it? It's everything that's most alive," Jean said.

"One thing is clear enough. The idea is that Death can return to life on this holiday, and this scene is one in which I can almost believe the dead return. They only need to follow the pied-piper dancing everywhere."

"We're nowhere near the end of it and it's already beyond words."

They decided to walk over the bridge and see how the palaces were celebrating the Day of the Dead. They sat at a table outside an upscale cantina and watched the processions and dances passing by. They expected the energy to abate but, incredibly, it did not. A waiter in a skull mask came to serve them. "The liqueur of Death, please, for both of us," Red said. The skull face nodded right and left playfully and left.

"What on earth have you ordered for us?"

"Death only knows," Red said, smiling. "I'm starting to get into the spirit of this thing." Two bottles of tequila arrived with glasses and sugar skulls on the side. As the waiter opened the bottles and poured, he added a ripple of red food coloring to their drinks.

They all laughed. "Imbibe of death, my dear. It's part and parcel of the love of life today," Red said. They clinked their blood-red glasses and tasted rich Mexican tequila. In the street just beyond them, a huge skull with a body costume bearing a pink heart and wings danced about, blowing kisses to all. A King of Death was carried in an ornamental chair by skeleton slaves, his face a silver skull and his crown a golden sphere of skulls. He touched as many observers as possible with a skeleton scepter, and even Red was touched. "Apparently, I must drink and breathe my last," Red said.

"It's different across the bridge, though, isn't it?" Jean asked.

"Yes, I was thinking that, too. Suddenly I'm reminded of Gay Pride Day. They're re-interpreting the holiday, not dancing the sacred dances, making it something more like Carnival or Halloween. They've lost the stories, the myths; they've lost their beliefs."

"Should we go back to our peasants on the other side of the bridge?"

"Yes, after I finish my quaff of blood. They'll be going out to the cemeteries soon, if they're not there already."

THE CEMETERY LOOKED ancient, like American eighteenth-century churchyards: slender stone tablets without ornamentation and tilted at many different angles by the earth and time. Immediately, they spotted the three girls dancing solemnly beside the graves and their mothers not far off—Rosa, Blanca and Josefina—selling their goods as fast as they could move. Altars to the dead were everywhere, and graves were already receiving food. Death now wore enormous hats with monstrous flowers. It was covered with ribbons and bows, as though a gift to someone. Dead Elvis was dancing and singing in Spanish with his guitar, his great dark pompadour and sideburns hugging a skull with green and yellow stripes.

Jean suddenly saw a costumed figure that did not seem to fit in with the others. It was dancing elaborately among the graves with the dexterity of an accomplished dancer, but its movements made no sense at all. It was clearly not engaged in a sacred dance. It jumped in the air, only to wave its arms as though repelling something. It took small mincing steps, then great leaps, arms akimbo, and traced a chaotic invisible pattern. Then it stood perfectly still at an odd angle and began another run of equally bizarre movements that suggested nothing but dismay and alarm. It jumped to show its back, then slowly extended its trembling limbs as though in pain. It caressed the headstones, rubbed its genitals on them obscenely, took the graveyard as its dance partner. It was the least harmonious dance possible, evoking only horror and fear, delight and suffering at once, a creature that had completely lost its sanity. Its mask was strange, too— chaotic with three piercing eyes of different sizes and a mouth that was a vertical slit, as though it perceived so great a terror that it could not cry out. It was covered on the forehead, cheeks and chin with photos of women lying limply on the ground. As it moved closer to the crowd, it appeared that the photos showed dead women, and they covered its chest as well.

Voices were now raised as many people saw the strange dancer. Then a shout was heard and some men raced toward the figure. Others joined them, and all suddenly disappeared into the forest surrounding the cemetery. All eyes were upon the forest, and the women talked nervously, loudly, venting their fear as anger. After a breathless moment, the men began to walk back to the crowd. The dancer had clearly eluded them. They looked angry and defeated.

"What on earth was that?" Jean whispered.

"A dancer whose mask and chest were covered with what looked like dead women, probably the murdered ones, and he just got away, dammit!"

A loud, angry discussion followed among the revelers at the cemetery. Some were certain the photos were of the murdered women, others were not. Rosa and Josefina were holding their daughters and talking at once. The debate continued, some declaring that only the murderer could have those photos, others saying they were fake. The atmosphere had utterly changed. A different face of Death hovered over them—Death the destroyer, time's last thief, the one to be feared above all else.

Suddenly a great mad shriek came from the forest. The masked dancer was high up in a tree, his hand clutching his throat, shrieking at the crowd. His cry was again without sense or pattern except for its stridency and volume. Again, it displayed suffering and delight as one. It was utterly inhuman, alone, incomprehensible but for the shock of its presence. Two men ran back toward the forest. The figure leaped effortlessly to another tree and vanished. Wordlessly, the crowd sensed it could never be captured.

"My god, what do you make of that?" Jean asked in awe and shock.

"Someone who is completely mad but gracefully so, with some impressive dance training. That or a thing from another world, and I'm favoring the latter right now," Red said.

"Let's go home. I've had all I can take of that thing." They were completely silent as they walked in the direction of their home, then they stopped at a *grocería* for tequila and sat on a stone outcropping. "And, damn it all, I still don't know if it's true," Red said. "Not even the villagers are sure. Damn! Something so weird is going on here."

"Beyond weird. I would say evil but it doesn't make even that much sense. It's another way of torturing women: not knowing what you're up against."

"And my god, there's still another day of this . . . holiday."

When they returned home, they found all three women and their daughters talking softly together. They smiled at one another gratefully to see that all were safe. Red and Jean didn't even attempt to ask them their impressions. It was getting late and they immediately separated for the night. Red and Jean held one another in bed and said nothing more, letting sleep and the dark take them far away.

In the morning, Jean was the first to awaken. She was sweating and felt strangely exhausted, then remembered that she had been running away from something in a nightmare but could not recall any details. Hot and humid, the day pressed against her roughly even as it glowed almost voluptuously on the weeds, Yucca and pine trees outside the window. A scattering of light and heat, the day was a multiplicity of living things and sensations oppressively beyond her control, a force that could touch every part of her body and mind. It is awful, she thought. I always have nightmares when it's hot. She heard a piercing cry and what looked like a blazing cobalt blue dagger, a hawk with a rabbit in its claws, suddenly soared into the sky, gliding close to the windows on the second story. Odd, those windows almost seem to have some power to attract, she thought; this only further jangled her nerves. It will pass, she thought. I'll feel better again. I'll be with Red and the others.

Nieves suddenly wandered into the kitchen and sat at a table looking at Jean. Instantly, Jean felt delight. She had never been alone with this shy, sensitive child before and wondered what lay behind her huge eyes that so often reflected unhappiness. "Well, good morning," she said. "I was just wishing for some company. I was up first, so I'll make breakfast. What would you like?"

Nieves smiled. "I was lonely, too. Please, can I have beans, tortillas and milk? My mother always makes me that."

"I can do that but remember, it's a holiday and we can have fruit juice and eggs with cheese and ham. Would you prefer that?"

"Oh, yes!" Nieves said. "And maybe there's another sugar skull."

Jean found a plate of bright purple sugar skulls in the refrigerator and placed them on the kitchen table. "Just one before breakfast," she said. "Then some more after." An intuition suddenly flashed into Jean's mind: the women won't talk about the murders but a child might. She instantly felt guilt at the thought of manipulating a child but countered it with the thought that her intention was wholly to protect them all. She was unsure of nearly everything regarding the murders, but of that she was certain.

She smiled at Nieves and poured her a glass of orange juice. "It may take me a minute or so to make the breakfast, so why don't we play a game? Guess what I'm thinking? What could it be?"

"That's easy. You're thinking you had a good time yesterday, that the dead were a lot of fun to play with, and we still have another day to play with them."

"Yes, that's right," Jean said, and noted that Nieves had not understood the significance of the dancer and the women had kept it from her. "It's my turn. Let me see now. You must be thinking of yesterday, too. Your favorite things were the dancing and the sugar skulls. You also saw something that made people angry and scared."

"Oh, yes!" said Nieves. "They were very mad at him. His mask was wrong and he didn't dance the right way so they chased him away. But we all ate our favorite foods and were happy and there's still plenty of sugar skulls left."

"Well, I'm glad for that. Yes, the bad dancer made people think of sad things like the murders. Nieves, do you know any of the women and girls who were murdered, like the ones on Blanca's *ofrenda*?"

Nieves was silent and the black fire of misery flooded her eyes again. Jean felt an intense pang of guilt, remorse and empathy. I'm always on shifting round here, she thought. There's nothing I can do right. "One was my sister, my twin," Nieves said. "I miss her so much!" Her eyes were full of tears; yet, like most children, she could still eat her sugar skull. "My mother thinks she still might be found. She thinks about that a lot. But, I know. I've always known what my twin feels, not everything, but the simple things like whether she's happy that day. She was alive for one day, very scared. The next day I couldn't feel her anymore. She was dead. I know it." Nieves stared up at Jean with all the misery of childhood in her face—its helplessness, its intense emotions that could not be rationalized or repressed. Jean sat beside her and held her like a mother. She felt the small body relax and then three little brown fingers reached for another sugar skull. Jean smiled and soon after she rose and prepared their breakfast.

When Red and Jean were walking to the cemetery, Jean said, "I had a talk with Nieves early this morning before anyone else was awake. I know why that child is so terribly sad and shy, so unlike Teresa and Clara."

Red stared at her in fascination. "Out with it."

"One of the murdered girls was her own sister, an identical twin."

"My god, that's awful! How did it happen? What do they know?"

"She vanished, and a child that young doesn't walk long distances. So, between that and the madman yesterday with the photos, I'd say the murders are real. It's *true,* and we're right in its path!"

"We're in someone's path, but I'm not sure whose and why. Someone definitely wants to spread fear—but death, that I'm not so sure of."

"Then what happened to Nieves' sister, and what's going on with all the rumors of murdered women and girls?"

"I don't know, but there are a number of things here that don't make sense. First, that *thing,* that dancer yesterday was being awfully public about the murders, making a real announcement. Too, he can't be from this side of the bridge. Who has the money to train a son to dance? If *he* is the murderer, he's either from one of the palaces or somewhere else entirely. He could even have been hired to perform. Hasn't it occurred to you that *we* might be causing this? We're giving shelter to women from the community and sometimes letting them direct the builders. It annoys the builders, and it might just piss off some other men around here, too. They might be trying to scare us—into abandoning the women or even leaving, giving them the house. This situation is awfully complicated, to say the least."

"Yes . . . that's true. But we know that Nieves' sister disappeared and it was in the context of other disappearances and murders. *And* some community men might very well want to be rid of us. We're still right in the path of it."

"But of what, we don't know."

"That *was* a madman we saw yesterday."

"Definitely a madman or a 'mad scene,' I'll grant you, but with a disciplined dexterity the mad don't have, someone like an acrobat from a circus, and giving a perfectly timed performance. If you want to continue killing, you don't draw attention to yourself like that."

"Provided you have control of yourself, which a serial murderer by definition has lost."

"We've traveled in a perfect circle," said Red, "and it leads directly to this cemetery." They had just arrived at the cemetery for the final day of the holiday, and they felt relieved at last, protected by their uncertainty. A banquet was in progress all around the grave sites and everyone was eating and drinking tequila. There were only subtle, infrequent signs of yesterday's disturbing performance, Red noted, eyes looking up suddenly with a different expression and occasional looks into the forest. The dead have found their way home, Jean thought; it is a family holiday, all feasting and remembering. The dead deserve this: the Indian life has its own real wisdom.

"This is lovely," Red said. "In a way, it makes me think of Japanese cherry blossom viewing. Remember Tanazaki, *The Makioka Sisters*? We read that once together. Your annual viewing was supposed to be the deepest, most intense sense of the brevity of life. You needed it annually, and years could be compared in terms of how profound your experience was."

"I do remember that, but it was so much more cosmic; it was the brevity of all life, not particular people, and it was completely internal and emotional, like nostalgia. This celebration is so much more specific and external. It's raucous and colorful. The two practices are opposites, actually, but you're right in seeing that they achieve the same result. And, both acknowledge that we need an annual ritual sense of life's brevity."

"Let's sit here for a while." They were beside an old crumbling rock fence.

"Should we drink under imagined cherry blossoms like the Japanese?"

"I will certainly respond to that hint. You'll get your tequila, and we will combine our appreciation of the values of two wise cultures in our own perfect wisdom as American lesbians." They laughed and Red went in search of a tequila vendor, which was not hard to find.

When she returned with two bottles, Jean said, "This is our first Day of the Dead as Mexicans." Then they were silent, drinking and abandoning themselves to the uncanny power of a celebration of death. It was mid-afternoon and some families were starting to leave. Suddenly, Red looked up sharply. She spotted the same devil mask she had seen that night on the edge of the shantytowns. She felt a powerful impulse to run to the figure and tear its mask off. Enraged, she began to breathe heavily. But how strange, she thought, it would look to the other Mexican families, perhaps a desecration of their holiday. All were free to wear masks, after all. The masked figure was turned toward her, obviously watching and perhaps enjoying her frustration. She took a deep breath and tried to remember everything she could about its appearance. The figure seemed to be taller and stockier than the dancer, a different person, though she could not be certain. She gave it a look of hatred, which welled up in her again powerfully; she was shocked by its power. So I do believe it, all of it, she thought; that's my gut talking. "Let's go," she said to Jean. "That's enough." She looked at the figure again and left, knowing it would remain, with unknown and ominous consequences.

At home, they found the three Mexican women, all organizing the remainder of their goods from the holiday and their daughters washing the white paint off their faces. They were all nearly finished, and Clara suddenly rushed to Red and said, "Take us out in your car! We're done with the scariest stuff, so we want to speed really fast in your car on the highway."

"That does follow, doesn't it?" Red said. "Too much sugar on a holiday must be followed by too much speed on a highway. You aren't planning on screaming out the windows or anything like that, are you?"

"Of course we are!" Teresa said. She and Nieves had joined them.

Jean and Josefina were laughing. "Take them," Jean said. "We're running out of groceries, and I'd like to take the shopping cart and buy some more in town. I'll see you all later."

"Apparently, I am being kidnapped by children and forced to speed on the highway," Red said. "Oh well, it's a holiday. Let's see how dangerous we can be."

Nieves, Clara and Teresa were soon being driven by Red out of the small town on a dirt road. Red planned on reaching the highway, then driving at the speed limit. "Oh, no!" shouted Clara suddenly. "We should stay on the dirt road so that we can have clouds of dust following us. It will look like a great big caterpillar." There were murmurs of assent to this.

"I've always wanted to see that!" Teresa said. "*Now* go as fast as you can. We'll all look out the rear window and see how big a storm we can make."

"There are problems on dirt roads," Red said. "Animals use them, too, so we can't go fast. We might hit a donkey or a lamb."

"Oh, then we can nurse the lamb back to health!" Clara shouted.

"We'll take it home and nurse it," Teresa continued. "I'll pet it and feed it all the time."

"I'll put a cold cloth over its forehead," Nieves said. "It will sleep with me, so it will never be afraid."

"*I* get to sleep with the lamb," Clara said angrily. "*I* thought of it!"

"We'll nurse it for a long, long time," Teresa said. "It will be so happy and grateful."

"We can give up school to take care of it," Nieves said.

"Oh my," Red said. "No, kids, the lamb just won't see it that way. It will not enjoy being hit by this car and then leaving its mother to be nursed by you. *And* you have to go to school. *And* there are people working in the fields who don't like to breathe in dust storms. So, we won't do any of it, even though it's a holiday."

The three girls sighed.

"Any place you want to go?" Red asked.

"To the highway, then," Teresa said. "I want to see a really, really big bridge. I've never seen one."

Red turned gratefully onto a highway. "There are bridges stretching over highways. We'll find one soon enough."

"No, we've already seen those," Clara said. "We haven't seen the really big ones that go over rivers."

"That's for another trip," Red said. "We don't have time to find a river."

"Then I want to see one of those really tall buildings," Nieves said, "like in photos of big cities. The kind that can fall on top of you."

"So that's it," Red said. "You really want to see a big building fall on top of you. Actually, they're made very carefully to stand tall and never fall on people. That's why people are willing to live and work in them. I can't even drive you to one in time. That's for another trip. You have to get back for dinner and your homework tonight. You can't take long trips to rivers and big cities."

Red began to drive faster. "Now, look at this. We're going very fast."

The girls were silent, watching the land shoot past them. "This is the fastest I've ever been," Nieves said.

"I've been faster," Teresa said.

"Can we scream out the windows now?" Clara asked.

"Oh, yes," said Red. "Lock the doors first, then scream your lungs out." The three girls threw their arms out of the windows and screamed as loud as they could.

Good thing there's no one on this road, Red thought. I hope this finally wears them out. I should be back with Jean. It was dumb to leave her alone when that thing in a mask is free to go anywhere without being recognized. I can't do anything without thinking it through now. The ground keeps shifting on me. Red began to feel that prickling on her neck and then uncontrollable fear gripped her. She felt cornered, hunted, though the land was streaming past. She quickly took the next exit and reversed direction. I've got to get back there as fast as I can, she thought. She pushed the accelerator to the floor and roared down the highway, oblivious to the speed limit. The girls, thrilled, began to scream even louder. Holy shit, Red thought, it's the Wailing of the Damned to the rescue!

JEAN WAS WALKING into town with her shopping cart. She felt calm, light, and young in spite of the heat, and the pageantry of the day continued to beguile her. What was it all? she thought. It was gaudy sugar skulls, the living room full of women and their colorful art, the joy of children, dancing under the moon, and feasting among tombstones. They were beginning to love the place, in spite of the rumors. The Indians were right: nothing is entirely good or bad. This was life, and it should be celebrated. How many fiestas were there in the year? She had no idea. Many, no doubt.

As she approached the village, she saw a thick copse of trees she had never noticed before, a bit of the forest reaching into the town. The trees seemed to be deliberately planted and there was something behind them, something symmetrical and made of bright stone. She left her shopping cart on the dirt road and walked into the trees to see what was there.

It was a natural spring surrounded by a low rectangular rim made of pure marble; it glowed with life like perfect, young flesh. The water was green but reflected the sky in a sheen of blue; it was turbulent, as though it were the surface of a hot spring that ultimately passed deep into the ground. She knelt and touched the water's surface. It was much warmer than the day and even bubbled in places. How lovely and what a surprise, she thought. She could see caverns in its depths; it looked more and more like an entry into the earth. She wondered if the spring, in its depths, eventually met the sea. How close were they to the gulf? Close enough, she thought.

Something sparkled on the stone beneath the water. It was probably quartz, she thought, but toyed with the idea of precious stone, even gold. A chamber of mystery, a treasure, she thought. How right it was to surround it with marble, for nature to ornament itself. That, too, suddenly seemed part of the Indian wisdom. Who came here to love the spring? For whom was it beautiful? she wondered. There were thickening trees beyond it, the forest continuing all the way to the cemetery. Was it related in some way to the cemetery? she wondered. Did the Indians perceive symmetries between life, death, and nature that she and Red had never thought of? She saw something move in the forest beyond. What animals lived here? She was suddenly endlessly curious.

She walked further into the forest and confirmed that it was part of the forest surrounding the cemetery. She felt no fear. This was a world in miniature, a perfect harmony, a secret relation between what she knew and what she did not. And, what was life if not the discovery and understanding of such relations? She continued walking. The trees began to thicken and she considered going back and sitting beside the spring, perhaps taking her shoes off and feeling the warm, bubbling water on her feet and legs, even slipping into the water and finding out what the sparkling stone was. She began to walk back to the spring.

At that moment, she heard sounds behind her, subtle, careful steps on foliage. She turned and saw a figure that was distant and pale but for its head, which seemed to be masked. Suddenly, the world that had so tantalizingly opened itself to her seemed to rush inward and clutch her, trap her. She was breathing hard and she began to run. She heard someone running after her, far behind. But, he must be younger and stronger than she was, of that she had no doubt. How could she stay ahead?

She ran faster and lightning thoughts came into her head: move chaotically, in no pattern that could be understood; don't run directly to the road, since it was too obvious and she might not be able to reach it first; run in a circle so no strategy could be known, a circle that emptied onto the dirt road. If necessary, scream but not right away since it used breath. Was there no tree wide enough to hide her? Could she still climb a tree? She ran faster, zigzaging, picked up a stone, and ran further. At last, a broad tree emerged. She stopped and hid behind it, the stone in her hand. The figure ran past, leaped into the undergrowth, and continued running. She saw that it was a naked man in the chaotic mask that she had seen before.

Perhaps she was safe, she thought. The dirt road was not far. She had not lost her sense of direction, and she had the stone. She reached for her pocketknife and opened it with as little movement as possible. Now she had two weapons. Her thoughts, previously as fleet as an animal, stopped. She breathed heavily and every part of her body seemed more alive than she had ever known it to be, enflamed, utterly unique. She was ready for anything. At that moment, she could kill the man who had chased her—quickly and deviously. He was stronger, but his mind was damaged. Hers was brilliant. She no longer felt herself at a disadvantage. She could murder as he could, as he had, like a savage, like an Indian. That, too, was right and wise.

At that moment, she heard Red's voice calling to her from the dirt road. Her lover was beside the cart, trying to find her. Jean screamed in joy and ran directly to Red. Then, she was clinging to Red, dropping her stone and knife. She was breathing hard and realized she was completely disheveled and wild, covered with dirt and sweat. Then three little girls were with them, still screaming as loud as they could.

"Oh!" Clara finally shouted. "We went so fast! We've never been so fast, and we made a dust storm as big as a dinosaur!"

"Yes, yes!" Nieves yelled. "It was more fun than anything!"

My god, Jean thought. I am an Indian squaw with my brood of Indian children and my brave beside me. She looked Red in the face and both knew that something terrible had happened. Slowly, they walked to the car arm in arm, then Red returned for the cart and put it into the trunk. For the moment, they said nothing about what had happened, instinctively protecting the children from something they could not understand.

"I've never had so much fun!" Teresa said. "We couldn't get Red to speed the car, then she turned around and drove back like a diablo!"

As Red put her key into the ignition, they heard an animal cry from the forest.

A man with a visible hard-on was screaming high in the trees, completely naked but for the chaotic mask they had seen earlier on the cemetery dancer. Suddenly, both Red and Jean believed that he was the killer of women and girls, and they felt murderous. They opened their doors and looked at the man, then at each other. Without a word, they knew that together, they could kill him, even in front of children, and they walked rapidly toward the tree from which the man had screamed. With the high shriek of an animal, the man jumped to another tree and vanished.

Belatedly, Red tried to remember everything she could about his body. He was slight of build, very small but with young, perfectly developed muscles, clearly the dancer from the cemetery but not the taller, stockier man she had seen later in the diablo mask. Were there two of them, she wondered, even a cult? With that, rational thought returned to them. They looked at one another and knew that they must talk at home, all night perhaps. Which is stranger, Jean thought, breathing deeply, that a madman is following us, or that I intended to kill him with my bare hands? That we both did?

"What was that?" Clara asked.

"A bird," Red said, "very rare around here."

"It looked like a little devil man and its beak was in the wrong place," Nieves said.

"Yes," Red said, "a very, very rare bird in these parts. Don't tell anyone about it. It's a bad omen, and if you never tell anyone about a bad omen, it can't hurt you."

The girls were suddenly very serious. They had heard about bad omens.

The landscape could not have looked stranger to Jean and Red as they arrived home. Trees, grass, vines, clouds, their own breath, seemed full of threats, signs, and messages. The Yucca tree with its strange white leaves and its few thick, curved branches looked like muscular wrestlers throwing their arms into the air in ominous triumph. The Mexican pine trees with their slender, reed-like clumps of leaves looked, in the wind, like a group of greenish blue sprites all shaking their witch-like hair at them. They heard the high, rolling *craak* of a wild parrot and flinched as though it had been gunfire. They stood and waited as though their lives depended upon reading signs. Suddenly, they heard the slow, wobbly tread of an invisible creature beyond the trees, probably an opossum, they thought. Breathing deeply, they held one another, then entered their home. The girls had already run into the house and were exclaiming over what fun they had. Good-lord, Jean thought, I've never been closer to death and more alive, and damn the thing for its god-forsaken beauty! The Day of the Dead indeed! They both took a handful of purple sugar skulls from the plate as they went into their bedroom and closed the door.

"Alright," Red said, eating a sugar skull at once. "Let's take it from the beginning. What on earth happened? Do you know what that damned thing wants?"

Jean began unsteadily, rationally. The ground was shifting everywhere, but stories were real, and she could tell this one.

In the living room, Clara said angrily, "Red and Jean took *all* the sugar skulls that were left! Now there aren't any more for us."


IN THE MORNING, Red and Jean awoke from a short, fitful sleep after talking for half the night. They agreed that what had happened was incomprehensible but for a few hints: the hot spring and the murders might be related to the practice of human sacrifice. The deep springs, Red said, were one of the sites of the ancient Indian sacrifices; not all were carried out on the tops of pyramids. There was a stronger suggestion of the participation of more than one man, and it might represent a secret cult or a group of shaman in the area, particularly given its association to the hot spring, the fiestas and the ancient religions. Most of the fiestas were related directly and indirectly to the fertility of the land, Jean observed, and the ancient belief was that the sun and thus the land and the earth itself could not continue without the shedding of human blood. They agreed that the strange man who haunted the forests was clearly insane, though the motives of the other man or men involved were less clear and might even be related to them and their effect on the community.

A relation between the fiestas and the murders would be a terrible blow to the community even beyond the death of one member, they reasoned, since the fiestas were family holidays that cemented communal bonds. This would account for the anger and fear expressed by both men and women. They considered themselves to be in a confusing position, since what they knew was hearsay; they had not actually seen any crime. They could not police the forests, the spring and the cemetery, though people in positions of authority should clearly be doing so. This lack of basic civic protection was very ominous, they thought. Too, they continued otherwise to love the house, the Indians and the town; and they were acutely aware that their retirement savings were now intertwined with them.

They decided to find out, first, why no other authority like the police or the government had apparently investigated the murders. For this, they must talk to Rosa, Blanca and Josefina, though the ideal time would be in a day or two, since they had all just celebrated a holiday in which the murders were vividly brought to everyone's attention at the cemetery. They must insist on knowing, in spite of any opposition.

Red awoke first and made coffee, eggs and toast for herself and Jean. The others had already left the house for school and work.

Red drank her coffee alone and looked out at the construction, noting that the men were working well after a two-day holiday but had become acrimonious again. She suspected hangovers and the heat as the cause and listened to the many conversations going on outside. Then she heard something that made her feel as though someone had just punched her in the gut. She poured a cup of coffee immediately for Jean and returned to the bedroom with breakfast. Jean was awake and smiled at her lover.

"Breakfast in bed, served by one to whom it is anathema. Can you be in a good mood after so much midnight talk and so little sleep?"

"Ah, that," Red said and looked away. When her eyes returned, Jean saw so much love and sorrow in them that tears came into her own eyes.

"It can't be," Jean finally said.

"Ah, yes, it can. It's the main topic of conversation out there: another murder of a woman last night. Now they sound certain; it's more than a rumor. Rosa and Blanca must have left to get more information. When they've all returned, sometime tonight, we must insist that they tell us everything."

"I wonder who she was," Jean said. "I hope it was not a girl, a childlike Nieves' sister."

Red's eyes now teared as well, but she said, with effort, "Enough until we know more. Now, enjoy the spectacle of me serving you breakfast in bed. I still think it's the height of decadence, but it's the only thing I could think of to do with myself."

"We can make the noon feast for the builders."

"Rosa and Blanca should be back by then; the girls next, then Josefina will be here last. Rosa seems to be the most directly involved, but I really want to know what Josefina thinks. That's one bright, tough woman. I bet nothing gets past her."

ROSA AND BLANCA returned at noon and made the feast for the builders. They seemed very restrained and inquired politely whether Red and Jean had enjoyed the holiday. They all made careful small talk with one another and waited for the others, a facade that was violated only by their concern over whether the three girls arrived home on time. They all spent time in their usual pursuits until Josefina arrived.

Her entrance was spectacular, since she brought two other women with her. The women, who looked frightened, were introduced as Pepita and Maria. Pepita was a diminutive woman in traditional dress and Maria, tall and elegant, surprised them all as the first woman in a business suit. Her hair was carefully styled and she wore make-up. Strikingly beautiful, her dark features were similar to Teresa's. Jean instantly said to them, "You are welcome to stay as long as you want," not even waiting for the question to be asked. "I'm not sure how comfortable you'll be with cots, hammocks and mattresses, but we will find some better way tomorrow."

The women murmured their assent. "It's how we all began with our families, many in one room. We have only to remember," Maria said.

"But we must talk to you about what is happening to women here," Red said. "We really must. We want to help you, and we'll be able to do it more effectively if we know what has happened here, apparently for some time."

Jean subtly gestured toward the girls. Blanca and Josefina immediately responded by asking their daughters to read and study on the second floor for an hour or two. The girls, who clearly suspected nothing, asked in excitement if they could light candles, look out the wall of windows at the night, and tell scary stories, then have a pillow fight in the hall. When this was granted, they ran up the stairs and were completely insulated from the conversation below.

"Candles are actually a good idea," said Rosa, taking the cross from around her neck and placing it on the living room mantle. She lit a nearby candle from Blanca's *ofrenda* and placed it beside the cross. "There is now one more to pray for," she said as she turned off the electric lights. The women all sat on the living room floor, which was comfortably carpeted.

"Would it help if I brought wine in for us?" Red asked. There were immediate murmurs and sighs of relief. Red went into the kitchen and brought glasses and two large jugs of regional red wine, which was placed at the center of their circle.

"Serve yourselves," Jean said, "as much and as often as you want." With their glasses full, the women looked at one another in the flickering light. First there was silence, which did not make them uncomfortable but, rather, partook of the wavering light's wordless power and became a positive force. They looked at one another more carefully and a truth began to take hold: that they would know what was happening and what to do; that they could and would protect one another; that they were strong.

The Mexican women were reminded of evenings spent by a fire in the villages of their parents, places even smaller and more remote than the town, times when stories were told and strength flowed from one person to another, times of trust between men and women, a time that had been lost. They had not thought of that for a long time, they reflected. How long ago was that, a time when men and women trusted each other? Had it ever really been true? they wondered. Probably not, but there was a time when they believed it; for, after all, they had once loved their fathers and mothers.

For Red and Jean, candles and wine meant music and conversations that went on long into the night and allowed them a complete and unimpeded sense of who they were and where they were going, together; for that could be easily confused in their world, too, even as they parted a curtain and looked out on a San Francisco street at night, shrouded in fog yet well-lit and clean beneath its secret torments and mysteries. There was that much these women held in common wherever they found themselves in all the multitudinous surfaces of this flickering, wavering world—death and life, clarity and mystery, trust and betrayal, men and women, minds full of love and minds full of violence, damaged beyond repair. There was always danger just behind them, and there was always the strength that seems to come at first, and then is inconceivably and most powerfully there, in whatever you call your being, at last. So you see, as a poet, I was there just as surely as they were, as you are, for that is my home, the insides of things, where it is dark but still a bit of light left for all, flickering as a candle does, wavering, changing before your hand, seen in half-light, moves before you in the most intense, breathless sensation and then one day vanishes, along with whatever truths and secrets it held. That's how I know the meaning of stories and how I know theirs.

"When did it begin?" Red asked.

Then they all began speaking at once. "It was always there—even my grandmother knew it—no, it is very new, since women have been working outside their homes—but then it stops, why just a week ago it was gone and then—" They all laughed, since they had been speaking at the same time. They knew they must begin again, one at a time.

"It's been here for a long time, I think," Rosa said with tears in her eyes. "Once, women lived longer than men here . . . then it reversed and at first, it seemed accidental. When it happened again and again, we were certain. But, it stops for long periods and we think it is over. Then, it begins again."

"Most often," said Blanca, "we can't find the bodies. The women disappear, but they are not the kind to run away. They were taken, like Rosa's daughter."

"What are they like?" Jean asked. "Are there more women than girls? Are some loners? Does he follow them for a time, pick them off? Do you think they know him?"

"No," Pepita said. "It is stranger than that. There is no pattern. They somehow cross paths with him, excite him. He goes a long time without killing, as though he slumbers, then he sees someone, either a woman or a girl. It feels supernatural, like a god waking up for some reason. We pray for it to stop, but it doesn't."

"Why haven't the police found him?" Red asked. "If there are so many victims, why isn't the government or the military involved? There should be national media attention and a manhunt going on, known well by everyone in the country, and here I don't even read a word about it in the newspapers."

"You must pay them to get any help at all, and the victims and the town are poor. The authorities are completely corrupt," Maria said. "And, they care much more about what happens to men than to women. Sometimes, I try to imagine what they're thinking. Maybe they think it's the husband, the lover or father, and he had his reasons. They would stop there, you see."

"What if I went to the police with the names of the murdered women and girls, gave them the heftiest sum of money I could, and asked them to find the murderers?" Red asked. "Would that do it?"

"Probably not, though I know you mean well," said Maria. "It's been going on too long and too many people know about it, people in power. You're not even a real part of the community, except to us. No matter how much money you have, someone with more doesn't want it known, or it wouldn't have gotten out of hand like this. Or, at least, that's what I make of it."

"Why didn't you want us to know, Rosa? Blanca?" Jean asked. "Why did you try to stop us from knowing?"

The room was silent for a long time. Outside, the wind was rising, and they heard the endless stirring of things living and dead: animals, trees, leaves, dust. At last, Pepita responded. "I can answer that. Finally, we fear *all* men. The police and the government are probably in on it. It can sleep and we want it to just stay asleep. You come from another world. You would try to bring in the police, the government. We have no faith in them, and they can make it worse. Just let it sleep because it will and we can be grateful for the time we have." The wind blew heavily outside, and they all heard the softest and most dangerous sounds of night creatures, moving and crying so faintly as almost not to be there, phantoms. But, they were there. It should have been a moment of beauty, Jean thought, of union with all that is. But it is agony, and death is the uninvited guest, moving in the room, a shadow we never know until it falls on us or someone else.

Red broke the mood, for it was her nature to resist. "We have seen two men we suspect," she said. "One is small, muscular, very adept in his movements, like someone trained as a dancer or an acrobat. He seems to haunt the forests around the cemetery and the hot spring. He was the dancer at the cemetery wearing that strange, chaotic mask, and we are certain that he is insane. We saw him the day after, too; he was following Jean in the forest. The other man we suspect is bigger and stockier, not athletic at all, clumsy, in fact. We have seen a diablo mask on him, just before the time when a woman is murdered. The bigger man does not show signs of insanity and might have other motives for killing. We suspect there may be other men as well, possibly shaman conducting ritual killings, like human sacrifice or even devil worship. Do you know these two men?"

"You've seen a lot in such a short time," Blanca said. "That could mean danger because you have been noticed, picked out. Those are the women he murders. Still, I think you are safe here, in this house. He has never taken a *gringa*, and he or the man he works with knows your government would retaliate, and he could lose the protection he seems to have here. You are right that there are *brujos*. A few are good men, but there are others and we know little of them. They don't want to be known, and it is better for you if you know little. Human sacrifice? I would believe anything of them. They are very evil, damaged, like the small man, who we have indeed seen many times. We call him the were-jaguar. The Olmecs believed that such a creature existed. The other man we know, too, but he could be anyone. We look for men with their builds and movements, but there are many, especially like the big heavy one."

"Josefina, what do you think?' Red asked.

"I don't put much thought into the supernatural—the sleeping god, the *brujos*, the were-jaguar—though yes, I have heard about them, especially around the fire or when candles are lit. I think we live in a world where no women have positions of power. I believe that is a violent, unjust, uncaring, corrupt and ultimately dying world. This is true everywhere, not just Mexico, and it will be true until women rise. Damaged men? Sure, there are plenty of them, but it is almost impossible to damage a woman in the same way. When my daughters are older —high school or college, I'm taking them out of here. I'm not sure where yet, but it will be safe. I will keep them safe in any way I can. That's why I'm here. I will fight for them, and they will be safe. The darkness in us all? Oh yes, it is very dark. But, *I* can't be stopped by anyone, man or god. My daughters are loved and they will be well educated. They will rise in this world, and so will their daughters. *This* you can believe!"

There was silence after this. "Ah," Pepita said at last, "if only I could believe that."

"There were desecrations found in the church later on," said Blanca. "Not all of you know that. The virgin had a noose around her neck, and there were *milagras* painted on tin of dead women and votive paintings of dead women bordered with paper flowers." To Jean and Red, she explained, "These are normally signs of gratitude. They are expressing gratitude for the deaths of women. That is why we think of the *brujos*."

"Are some of the women fighters? Do they challenge the male order?" Jean asked.

"Some have," said Josefina. "I am here for that reason, too."

"I, too," Maria said. "I have a small rental car business near the airport. I live a short distance from here. But, I come to see my mother and my brothers. I am concerned about their safety as well. There are more rumors than the ones you have heard," she said directly to Red. "The little jaguar is said to be a son of one of the wealthy families over the bridge. His mind is damaged and he is very dangerous, but his family has PRI connections and wealth. So, he is protected, and there is even more corruption here than meets the eye. The times when he seems to sleep might be times when he is in a mental hospital or restrained at home."

"I can buy guns and bullets for all of you," Red said. "After what has happened here, there would be no court, no matter how corrupt, that would fail to believe you did not have to act in self-defense if this man ever came after you. I can drive to a big city tomorrow and get them. What effect would that have? Would you feel safer?"

"I have a gun and bullets now," Maria said.

"So do I," said Josefina.

"So, Rosa, Blanca and Pepita, do you want guns?" Red persisted.

"Yes," they said.

"But I will not feel safe," Pepita said. "The killer uses a knife."

"How do you know that?" Red asked.

"The women who have been found. They were raped and roughed up, then killed with a knife. There were strange images carved on their bodies."

"But a gun would still have protected them. Are you saying he had some other way of overpowering them?"

"Anyone can kill another person, eventually," Pepita said. "Not on a particular day, perhaps, but eventually you sleep or you let down your guard or you are happy and forget. Don't we all want to forget?"

The room was silent, filled with a pulse of something dark, like the wind outside. "Ah, look, the moon," said Blanca. The women looked out the windows and smiled. The trees were bending in the wind and the clouds raced over the moon. "How can you not forget at times in a world of such sweetness, and how wonderful to enjoy it with women!" Amen, Jean thought. The pulse of fear and tension in the room began to abate.

Suddenly, they noticed that the group had a new member. Clara had just sat down on the stairs, quite close to them. Her hair was full of minute feathers and she had a tragic look on her face. "I lost the pillow fight," she said sadly.

The women laughed and their tension was dispelled. "Who is cleaning up the feathers?" asked Josefina in a voice not entirely empathetic.

"Teresa," said Clara, who looked miffed that they had laughed. "She won." She walked angrily back upstairs.

"So you see," Josefina said. "No supernatural, no hocus-pocus. The next generation, a child covered with feathers now but one day a woman full of accomplishments. I will keep them safe for that with every breath of my body!" Her face was proud, determined and fierce in the half-light but strikingly beautiful. There is the beautiful Teresa as an older women, Red thought.

"We are honored to be able to help you," Jean said. "This is what a life is for, to me. Ask anything of us."

Once again, their faces were bold and beautiful in the flickering light and once more, they thought that yes, they could understand it, that they could protect one another, that they were strong.

AGAIN, SOMETHING OF all the women mysteriously melded together, and they became fascinated with one another and spontaneous, sharing long histories and discovering observations and beliefs held in common. Pepita was a seamstress and sat with Blanca and Rosa in the living room, talking avidly while working during the evening, and Josefina and Maria returned to the house later. Red and Jean spent several hours talking with them and then returned to their own interests or one another. They also drove to a nearby city and bought firearms, bullets and additional mattresses and hammocks for the household as well as moving the women's belongings to the house. Red bought a gun for Jean, too, and taught Jean as well as Rosa, Blanca and Pepita how to use their guns, keep bullets handy and improve their aim. They did not mention their fears again. On the last day of target practice with Red, they even laughed at the thought of becoming *bandidos*, brandishing their guns. So, the group became self-sufficient together and the house became a home.

Soon, Nieves would undergo a religious coming-of-age ceremony performed at church when girls reached the age of

fifteen, the *quinceañera*. All the women planned on attending as
well as holding a small fiesta at home. Blanca was busy making
decorations for the church, and Pepita and Rosa collaborated on
making an elaborate white dress for Nieves.

On the day of Nieves' ceremony, the women walked on
foot to the small wooden building that had a primitive steeple
and served the needs of the town with a pastor who traveled
between several remote villages and their congregations. He
was present solely for ceremonies and confessions; the town
held its Sunday services without him, together singing, praying
and giving thanks for blessings they had received. The town
looked forward to the presence of a priest, a ceremony and the
opportunity for a confession, and the women looked forward to
Nieves' excitement. She had become much more confident as
a result of her close contact with Clara and Teresa, who always
seemed fearless and inventive to her. Her expressive dark eyes
reflected excitement far more than misery now, and Rosa was
elated by the change. She held a drawing of her daughter made
by Blanca bordered with paper flowers that she intended to leave
at the church as a votive offering her thanks for this unexpected
transformation in her daughter.

As Red and Jean sat on the simple rough hewn wooden
benches and looked at the altar and decorations before them,
they were struck by their humble simplicity and the deep
emotion elicited by that fact alone. The image of the Virgin
Mary and the Christ child looked very much like plaster
dolls that had been dressed in satin clothes by children; they
could hardly be called sculptures at all. Blanca's decorations
were no more than new ribbons for the altar and white paper
streamers forming billowing arcs over the roof's bare wooden
ceiling. Nieves approached the Christ child and placed one of
her favorite marbles and a tiny papier-mâché kitten at his feet.

Many other children had left their toys for the Christ child to play with. Other members of the congregation left wild flowers and small ribbons for the Virgin Mary.

The altar itself was no more than a small rudimentary table of old unfinished wood and a similarly crude cross that held up some worn red fabric bordered with gold thread and covered with embroidery of Catholic religious symbols as well as Indian symbols of the Aztec sun, moon and stars. A few candles had been lit before it, and an old and worn white cloth with holes covered the table. Nonetheless, the simple fact of this homely design brought a deep sense of peace and gratification to the crowd, which Red and Jean found very moving. This configuration, as old and impoverished as it was, spoke volumes of words and good will toward the world in spite of its want and injustice; and the two women looked at one another and smiled, each aware of their mutual appreciation of this unexpectedly exquisite demonstration of the most primitive courage and beneficence in the face of adversity. Red rose, took a tin *milagra* of the dark-skinned Virgin of Guadalupe out of her pocket, and placed it before the altar.

Jean smiled and looked at her in surprise. When she returned, she whispered, "You have no religious beliefs at all."

"I know," Red said. "It just seemed right to add another dark woman to the scene. Blanca painted it for me."

The altar was made more majestic by the room's lack of lighting, and its diminutive simplicity and humility, bordered by sumptuously empty shadows, pointed powerfully to another reality beyond it. The priest entered the room from the shadows on the left of the altar, bade them all sit, led them in a hymn, and then beckoned Nieves to join him at the altar. The ceremony was performed, and Nieves' duties as a woman, wife and mother were intoned and explicated.

At that moment, something seemed to enter the shadows and speak without words from the darkness, something ancient and abhorrent. All of the women felt it, believers and non-believers alike. The priest, a tiny man with the heavily creased Indian face of one who saw only vicissitudes in life, was describing such a limited, circumscribed condition that they all sensed an influence hostile to life in the room. The women's eyes lowered in submission or anger, and the men's glowed and followed the priest's words. The priest's voice rose to a high whine as he described the perils and punishment of any woman who failed in her humility and submission to men and their god.

Once again, that look of misery and helplessness filled Nieves' great eyes. The women were silent but resentful. Red and Jean wondered whether the priest was expressing his personal views or if the ceremony was in fact the one that all girls must hear. Jean looked at Clara, Josefina, and Teresa. Their eyes were fixed in rebellion upon the priest's face; they clearly accepted no submission. As Red looked around the room, she noted that all of the women sheltered in her home did not lower their eyes; that the other women did so with anger, grief or the deep crevices of an unutterably pathetic fatigue on their faces; that the men looked proud and combative.

"It's turning into a funeral," Jean whispered.

"The oddest one I've ever attended," Red said.

When Nieves returned to Rosa, her mother held her protectively in her arms. There were tears in Nieves' eyes as she looked at Clara and Teresa. Clara immediately crossed her eyes, and Teresa blew out her cheeks. The misery vanished from Nieves' face, and a small smile appeared on her lips. The priest looked severely at Clara, who he had seen first, then he walked behind an old bleached wooden fence that functioned as a confessional covering. The congregation lined up for their confessions, and the women left with Rosa's arm around Nieves' shoulder.

As they walked outside and created a distance between themselves and the church, Red said, "Your funeral is now over, Nieves. You have risen from the dead and we will celebrate with ice cream and cake."

The women and girls all laughed, and Teresa commented, "It happened to Christ, too, and they never even gave him any ice cream."

"Maybe that's why he always looks so sad," Clara said. Then, in pure joy, the three girls all ran to the house, and the women walked as fast as they could.

"I guess, they'll start the party without us," Rosa said, breathless.

"Let's try to run, then," said Maria with a laugh. Rosa was very slow, Maria was fast and athletic, and Blanca fell awkwardly on the ground. Laughing, they helped her up and continued running.

"Since I am running to catch up with the former corpse, this is the oddest funeral on record," Red said as she passed Jean on the run.

"What are we running away from?" asked Jean, breathless.

"It's what we're running toward," said Red, "something like hope, a bit of freedom thrown in."

"We'll have to leave a votive of thanks for that!" said Maria, smiling and passing them both. Maria, it seemed, was the most athletic, and it was she who first found the three girls with ice cream already smeared on their lips. Nieves would ordinarily have carefully wiped it away with her napkin but today, she proudly made a mess.

'Hey, you're supposed to be a woman now," Teresa said with a smile.

"It's really all just a big mess," Clara said.

THE NEXT EVENT the women attended together was a political rally and fund-raiser for the PRI state governor candidate. It was held, inevitably, over the bridge. The women did not expect to be enlightened but, rather, to stay somewhat aware of the hypocrisy around them and perhaps to laugh. The audience was comprised mainly of the wealthy; nonetheless, many men and women from their side of the bridge were there, possibly because food and drink were to be served. The event was held in front of an elegant town hall and decorated with strangely luxurious flags; it contrasted all-too-sharply with the crude, barn-like structure that functioned as a church for the poor and had provided Nieves with her coming of age ceremony.

On a grandstand stood a podium that was soon taken by the first speaker to wild applause. He was a man in his sixties who was introduced as Javier Sanchez Ruiz, and he had the distinguished, self-congratulatory aid of the successful elder statesman. His face and entire bearing beamed as he introduced the younger candidate, who had an Indian's thick head of hair carefully combed back, but like his backer had features that otherwise could as easily have been Spanish or Italian. The younger man, his party's candidate and introduced as Rodrigo Perez, had a broad, muscular chest that seemed almost unable to fit into a business suit. Though tending to overweight, his movement and demeanor were meant to suggest great energy and strength. He frowned immediately to display his serious purpose and began speaking in martial rhetoric, giving no hint of any specific awareness of the audience.

His themes were as grandiose and masculine as his oratory—Mexico's revolutionary past with the PRI, its powerful new economy of petroleum, the honor of his country as more than equal partner to the US, his plans to reduce drug-related

violence and governmental corruption, his efforts to protect the
dignity of the family as a force against poverty. With fervor, he
complimented the city as a leading force in the dynamism of
modern Mexico and his sense of intimacy with the crowd now
became evident, though it applied solely to the wealthy. There
was nothing in his speech about opportunities for the poor,
how to create jobs for them or the improvement of the town's
civic and local governmental activity, including its dysfunctional
police force.

Red and Jean initially smiled. "How do they get away with
this drivel?" Jean asked.

"No journalists, no questions from the audience, stunning
tolerance for bullshit, and nothing else on the horizon," Red
said.

They ignored the speaker and looked around at the audience.
The martial rhetoric was highly effective with men, even the
poor; they were following the speaker's manner if not words with
intense concentration. The women from the wealthy side of the
bridge looked bemused. The candidate was being understood
as a foible of their menfolk, and they seemed to be perfectly
comfortable with his near-senseless assault of loud words.
Women who are bought and paid for, Jean thought, a category
she had never envied. The women who were living in the house
looked completely disgusted. The other women from their side
of the bridge looked down in grief and the terrible fatigue of
submission Red and Jean had first seen at the church.

Red was struck by their faces, since they seemed to be the
only people who were responding emotionally to the farce of
this candidacy. It was as though a powerful ray of light suddenly
shined upon them, alone, a light that I am long accustomed
to in writing poetry, but it was rare in Red's thoughts. At first,
their variety was most evident. There were Indian women in

traditional dress of long embroidered skirts and white blouses, and some with clothing so old and worn that it was impossible to place in any style or tradition. Many had symmetrically round, flat-brimmed hats; others wore colorfully crocheted caps. Some had slitted oriental eyes and the eyes of others were more open and Caucasian; their skins were of many subtle hues, no two entirely alike. Their hair was very thick—plaited traditionally for some, pinned up into their hats for others, leaving tangled rings of hair about the ears and neck. Some faces were oval and some were the typically heavier, more square Indian shape.

Their lips were dark and full, and here the faces began to merge into one for Red, the one I have taught myself to see, the truest, the one revealed by poetry. Their lips were dark and full since they had all tasted the brew of all that is lost, of perdition. Their eyes showed a single point of light in pure darkness, the light you see in a cave or at the bottom of a well, the light you are grateful for and bless without thinking, because it is the only light in the world. Red saw the single face full of dignity as nothing else around it, bent down as the body itself was bent. This face was old, dry and creased far before its time like tattered linen, all of its life and tireless effort completely negated by the world, refused but remembered in a flood, like the images that may pass before the eyes of the dying, more powerful and true than any as they are dissolved by death; the body solid but bearing downward as the eyes are, showing its awful weariness made exquisite by refusal to be anything but true; brutally enhanced by the solidity of the body's form; and again she saw the eyes for it is there the tale is told, the eyes without life and animation for all of this woman's value denied, of so little worth that she could be killed for sport, when she was the only strong one, the only worker, the only holder of the family together, the only truth-teller, the only one to feel this moment completely and

so, the great creases around the eyes that saw it and the mouth
that sustained it; the weariness that was an entire map of the
spirit, eyes of utter defeat yet still alive, still with their dignity
and honor, their flickering light, yet, of pride and hope for that
is only human, the eyes that perhaps in death see everything.

That was the face of the Indian woman. They do not even
look at one another for support; they have already fallen, and
their strength is now deep inside them, in the cave, at the bottom
of the well where you can never reach it, barely visible, never to
be acknowledged here, perhaps never in this life. If they could
be an element of nature, they would be mountains, mountains
of truth; so immense is their reality and so complete the world's
lies. This gathering of the wealthy was a little pile of kindling
sticks when placed beside the Indian woman. We need a great
painter to reveal her, Red thought. She is the only thing worth
seeing here, this woman in her monumental dignity in the face
of denial, violence, callous lies and trivia. Where is the artist to
paint her? This is too great a truth to pass away in absence of our
sight. Tears were now in Red's eyes. She could only look down as
they did. I wish I could paint, she thought.

Jean touched her on the arm. One by one, the women they
sheltered were leaving. There was to be something of a reception,
food to be shared, but they would not break bread with this. Red
and Jean looked at the women walking home one by one, the
girls again running far ahead, the children kept in innocence and
love, in childhood. Reality was a thing to be brought to them
gently, to a self that was already strong and free, unharmed and
protected before it must see the world, this face of the Indian
woman. So they all looked at them running and smiled. Red
looked at Jean, whose face was also covered with tears.

Why did I not see this before? they thought. It was there
in the church. I saw it but did not let it flood my being. And

they thought, we chose this in our youth and foolishly called it paradise, for that word creates visions, craves expression madly, has a life of its own beyond other words, and must be applied to something, somewhere, but it was true only of what they felt then and not of any place or time. Now we have come to it in age, and it is the reverse, the betrayal of all women. Yet we can live in it, for it is a revelation of truth and we are now made of it, as poetry shows us that we are made of our revelations as of nothing else. We thought we had come for its beauty, to pursue an ideal, but we are here for complete clarity, to see the entirety of this world, to see what the dying perhaps see, what a god would see if there were gods. This was worth it. It may be dark and full of danger but to see it was worthy of being human.

Again, we all return to the house, Red thought, to ideals and hopes, from what is farthest from the truth, and how strange that such a place as ours exists here, a shelter a just god would make if there were one, a thing that life demands or life will cease, almost as the ancient Indians believed.

# part two
## The Madman

IT WAS A few days before the Day of the Dead, and Carlos Cuevas Ruiz was taking his medication regularly and feeling more coherent by the day, almost by the hour, he thought. He had not heard any of his terrifying voices for nearly a week, and Dr. Molina had said his recovery was remarkable, as it had been in the past in his teens and when he was a university student. He was looking out of his bedroom window into the early evening, hot but windy and so alive. He loved the twilight; it was not a single entity or quality because everything moved: shadows; leaves; colors turning into darkness; the muted, curving glow around the fruit hanging from the trees of his father's estate; the inky layered clouds about the dying blood of sunset; the sounds of laughter (how different it was in the nightfall, suddenly ominous or erotic); the sigh of wind that was so melancholy and melodious at once; all precious things.

His family had such vast wealth; their home was palatial, but his grandfather, Javier, the state governor and PRI leader, and his father, Alvaro, a painter and sculptor, knew so little of what was precious. The world to his grandfather was an anomaly to be dominated and corrected to his taste and to this father, the torment of a wounded desire to create. His mother, who had also suffered from madness, had killed herself long ago. He, Carlos, was so different from them; only he could discern what was in this state of flux, purely alive, precious. Nothing is ever still, he thought. Everything in the world moves, changes, often becomes its opposite. He heard a soft, faltering step over the thick grass of his father's lawn. That must be old Antonio running the sprinklers. Only at night when it was cooler could they do their work effectively. Antonio walked with a thick, strong cane, slowly for his age, and the softness and delicacy of his frail movement nearly induced ecstasy in Carlos, now, alone in the dark.

What was its sound? A rare, strange thing that created no opposition, utterly smooth, velvet, ice, a girl's luminous, naked skin, down on a newborn animal: beautiful, precious things, all. He could feel them all the time and his father, who so needed them for his painting and sculpture, could not. That was Alvaro's particular pain, and as for his grandfather, nothing precious had ever entered the domain of his dominance and control. Carlos pitied them, both scorned and feared them, loved and hated them. But he, Carlos, was after all a madman; this fact made him laugh in a strange, agonized joy. He was partially sane at times, as now. He could not even remember his last period of pure madness. They told him it happened one night a short time ago. They implied that he had done terrible things and must take his medication carefully. They administered it, not trusting him to do so.

It was a strange but wonderful life, he thought. He really had two lives, this one that he loved and that other one he did not remember and they never described to him. He could feel from their distress, guilt, even terror, that he must have done awful things, changed in terrifying ways. But now, he was only Carlos, the beautiful, lucky young man who had recently graduated from the university and returned home, to their palace, a place of absurd luxury. His mad periods had begun in his teens and been infrequent but somehow always there in potential, blooming suddenly like a rider appearing against the horizon, inevitable, precious in its unpredictability and strangeness, its capacity for flux, turning the world upside down.

Before returning from the university, he could clearly remember his hallucinations and the full period of his mad spells. They were as clear and direct as a bell's ring, as sunlight, frightening to others but not to him. For then, in his hallucinations, the world became a living thing. He knew her name, even; the scientists called her Gaia. The world was a woman, a very beautiful one with whom he made love and passed into a consciousness wherein they were a single being. Then he knew all of the world's mysteries, secret processes, its most subtle states of energy and being. He felt the creation of everything—wind, rain, lightning, volcanoes, sunlight, chaos, darkness.

He knew the agony of thunder, for indeed it was a giant, muscular god whose limbs agonized as they rumbled together; he knew the cold, piercing shriek of lightning for it was so, that god shrieked as he lost his identity when the lightning of his limbs struck the earth and vanished again and again. These were all aspects of the rain god, Tloc, who he became and Quetzalcoatl, the plumed serpent who was lord of water, wind and earth. He knew the heat and explosion of being in volcanoes, spawn of lord Quetzalcoatl, for he was a god that agonized and shrieked at once, nearly dying, only to survive in pain and joy at once. He marveled at the passion and energy of these gods of whom he became a part in the intensity of his madness.

But he had been in union, too, with light, Huitzibpoctl, the god of sun and war, for to see was to be at war, to destroy, another form of this divine agony. He could feel this agonized light touching everything at once, and he was struck dumb at the breadth of its reach and power. That was a good god to be, stretching in all directions, limitless. But then, he also knew darkness and chaos, and they were even more beautiful: the Dark God Tezcatlipoca, from the ancient time of a lightless, shapeless earth. Chaos throbbed in an agony beyond any other. Its pain was thrilling to him; it was so much greater than that of thunder. This shapeless god must hurl itself in every direction at once, trying hopelessly to create a form and always failing. It invited him to join it and he did, marveling at how much it could kill, destroying both the form and meaning of all things. How terrible and marvelous was this god.

Creation and destruction were always followed by twilight and then darkness, a melancholy god, looking at a universe in which everything had been destroyed. It was silent, moving slowly. It was not dead, no. It was condemned to life, as was he, for there had been five suns and five earths, so this god still moved slowly and in it he could see what would become the great serpent, Quetzcoatl. And, the cycle would begin again and thunder reared up from the roiling mass of all that was. Perhaps he most loved the moment before the recreation, when all was dark and silent but moving, feeling its many possible forms, intensities, levels, meanings, all that could be and all that would be. He, Carlos, was a creature who was most alive here: its agony was greatest of all.

Yes, back then he remembered his astonishing hallucinations. Now, he would wake up, naked, remembering nothing at all, being washed by his father until he was clean and sane. There had been awful things on his body, probably cosmic signs and omens, enabling his father and grandfather to know that he had done terrible things. He remembered his father's face. It was distorted into such expressions of horror that it became a mask. His father had asked his grandfather to see him before he was washed clean, and the same mask of horror appeared on his grandfather's face. It was a mask Carlos loved, for all masks are sacred and beloved to the gods. Even now, he remembered nothing more than this of his last frenzy, waking up, in his clean bed and then taking the medications and their praise at his progress into sanity. But, he was still mad, of that he was certain. He was still the god Xochiquetzal, the Flower Bird, that so excelled in fleet and supple motion in the forests around the estate. That was still his natural domain, not his life in the palace with his family. This thought made him laugh long and hard. He would merely pretend to be like them; in fact, he was still a god, a darkly powerful and subtle one.

He walked through their home, the palace with bars over every window and door. That was not for him; they had always been there, like all the other palaces around them. His father and grandfather were now trusting him a bit, giving him the freedom to range throughout the house and even to walk around the lawn and orchard outside, no further. Thus, he walked like a god through his palace that was so full of priceless objects from the travels of his father and grandfather, marble floors and columns, thick Middle Eastern carpets, rooms so luxurious that every inch was covered with works of high art—Picassos, Matisses, Mondrians—little from his own country, though there were two paintings of Frida Kahlo and a huge Diego Rivera mural surrounding the swimming pool.

Each immense room of his palace seemed, to him, to be composed of many intimate atmospheres for infinitely subtle communications. In the living room, an Oriental section held fine ivory carvings of Kuan Yin and the Taoist Immortals, ancient watercolors from the T'ang dynasty. Another area held Medieval tapestries of saints in complex arbor-like wooden frames. A statue of pure gold showed a Greek sage in Renaissance garb, working at his desk. Behind it was a window of stained glass showing monks at work in gardens and Christ seated on a throne.

To his delight, there were some phases and corners devoted to Mexico; some were stark with huge, abstract paintings of no more than colored lines covering the entirety of the walls and on the floor humble pottery urns receiving the only sunlight. Other areas were full of brilliant folk art—masks of devils and other figures of folklore, elaborate tapestries and clay sculpted scenes of peasant and animal life, of which they knew so little. All this wealth was funded by the PRI through his grandfather, and it returned such favors through lavish parties for the wealthy that had been a part of his life since childhood.

His eyes swept the living room and he thought, what a perfect place for madness. He allowed himself the pleasure of a brief, insane laugh. It was unfortunate that his father and grandfather could not appreciate the madness of their boundless luxury. His grandfather Javier had always been too active in PRI politics, oblivious of all else. His father, Alvaro, was depressed and embittered over his recent inability to paint. Alvaro had even spoken angrily at the dinner table during one of his grandfather's PRI fund-raisers. He had said that he had seen nothing worth painting in all of Mexico. What, after all, could anyone at this dinner table name, he asked, and stared fiercely at them all in defiance. This was greeted with shocked silence, but for Carlos' own half-suppressed chuckle. His grandfather had been furious and later shouted in rage at his father, which only increased his father's despair. He, Carlos, continued to smile at their foolishness. Who was the greater embarrassment: the grandson, a madman who lived beyond reality, or the father, who spoke the filthy truth of reality? All three of them—grandfather, father and grandson—were monsters, he thought, and laughed again.

Continuing to move slowly through the palace, he suddenly caught sight of himself in a mirror. He was beautiful, of course. His hair was full and light brown, his skin the palest olive, his features European rather than Indian, except for his minimal height. Girls and women loved him easily and the family had somehow managed to keep his madness from exposure. His body was a perfect piece of Greek sculpture. The earliest sign of his madness had been a childhood diagnosis of hyperactivity. His father, in an effort to give his son's energy an outlet, had enrolled him in ballet lessons, but Carlos had found them emasculating and refused to continue. Then, they set up a huge gymnasium in the house and hired a trainer in acrobatics, martial arts and body building. That was the charm, activity he loved and practiced every day, and the strategy's success displayed itself in every moment of his perfect movement and musculature. For many years, his grandfather and father assumed that he would marry a beautiful, cultivated women of their class and continue the family line in many fortunate offspring.

But that had now changed, he thought with a smile. Now, they wanted him well hidden from the world and imagined him a prisoner. He was not, of course. He was capable of leaving anytime, but they did not know this and he surely would never reveal it. His eyes continued to move over the infinite spaces of art that covered every ceiling, wall and floor of their amazingly luxurious house. All these subtle atmospheres inherently generated by art were useless, Carlos thought. Their houseguests spoke of nothing but the PRI and its prospects. His father no longer invited his artist friends; he could not bear for them to see his despair and disgust. The house meant only power, the beauty that can be bought, the future of the PRI. It also meant corruption and brutality, but that was never openly revealed. So, all the art, all the subtle atmospheres, were invisible, wasted. How he would love to populate the palace with the far more intriguing creatures who whispered obscenities and visions of violence to him in his periods of pure insanity. How much more interesting, receptive, and appropriate they would be in such an atmosphere. Or, how much more appropriate it would be to fill the palace with the howling and roiling of the ancient gods he became in his visions. Art was a doorway to and a resonance of them, as close to their world as the sane ever got. How fitting, how much better it would be to have them here, leaping from the art and marble to confront these barely conscious people milling about, chasing them out onto the lawn, then tumbling all over the luxurious chairs and pillars, finally destroying it all! Though they would never destroy him, not Flower Bird, Xochiquetzal! How he and the gods would all laugh at this puny world and then, just for an instant, their agony would be relieved. He laughed out loud. Oh yes, such luxury was the abode of madness, even of great madness, for the house, too, had severed all relationship to reality. He had said this, only once, in front of his father and grandfather; and his grandfather, their great state governor, had slapped him across his face. And even then, he could not stop his mad laughter. He did not find this attack surprising. They all lived in a world of men, and that world was brutal.

But Carlos had his vengeance when his voices and hallucinations returned, as inevitably they did. He would become a god again, then many gods, and do whatever he pleased without judgement or punishment as befit the gods. He toyed with the idea that his PRI houseguests would approve; their own brutality was barely below the surface, their distance from the reality of others was as extreme as his, for they had that unique brand of madness known as politics. He was outside the house now and loafed on the lawn in a huge luxury chair, then he heard the low drumming that meant Diego wanted to see him. Diego was a friend from his childhood, and Carlos considered him to be a madman, too. After all, the fool dabbled in the black arts and had joined a group of *brujos*. Again, Carlos took the luxury of a mad laugh.

It was very dark now, and Carlos put on a grey unitard that he used when he wanted to move around the town at night, unseen. He had many of these garments hidden in the attic, and he always left by the attic window, which appeared to be locked but was not. Diego had jimmied it to ensure their continuing meetings and friendship. Halfway out the window, he caught a glimpse of himself in a mirror and noted the muscularity and perfection of his body. Perfect for what? he asked himself. For madness and violence, for godhead, he answered, and again laughed.

It was simple for him to jump from the roof to the nearest tree; and then, since the forest thickened, he could effortlessly jump and swing through the whole area using the boughs of the treetops and not touch the ground at all. In this way, he reached Diego's small shack invisibly. He could smell it, even high in the trees, before he dropped to the ground and walked toward it. The strange smell was given off by Diego's collection of herbs, chemicals and potions, burnt offerings, something vaguely mineral in scent, probably animal blood, and the candles and altar fires he tended year-round, even during the hot, balmy nights. When Carlos reached the threshold, he experienced an odd trick of the light: the moonlight seemed to revolve upside-down. Magic and madness, he thought and smiled. They are one.

When he entered the shack, his senses were further stimulated by Diego's colossal altar to the ancient Aztec and Mayan gods, particularly the Dark God and the devil. Carlos could only smile, for this was another perfect home for madness. I go from one madhouse to another, he thought, from politics to black magic and find but one reality. He laughed again even before greeting Diego, who had another shaman with him tonight, a small, wiry man with jerky movements and the large, small-pupiled eyes of vicious forest carnivores, which he resembled. The man had a strange, gleeful smile and seemed to be quite a madman, too. Carlos dropped casually into an odd flower-like chair made of forest reeds. The shack was just as he always found it—full of strong odors, faintly unpleasant, candles and fire, herbs, painting and symbols of the gods, hermetic images, hookahs and magic paraphernalia everywhere crowding the space, which was very small, only two rooms. One for sleep and one for the violence of consciousness, Carlos thought.

"We've brewed some very good mezcal," Diego said with a broad smile, "and we're so close to the Day of the Dead that we thought you'd like to share it with us."

Carlos only laughed again. "So again we all drink and become madmen together?"

"Why not?" asked Diego. "You know that you love it." The eyes of the small man (hunched over himself like a hamster), began to look larger and darker, tremulously glittering like a river at night. He found Carlos very beautiful, charismatic and fascinating in his unitard.

You look like a monkey about to touch a star, thought Carlos. What filth these *brujos* are. He felt his superior class status in an intense repugnance for both men. "Actually, I don't remember anything about my night with you, but I'm quite willing to believe that I love being even more insane than I already am. Why not? I'm a god. Is your mezcal going to stink as usual?"

"I'm afraid so," Diego said, "but after the first sip or two, you'll love it. It's the doorway to the gods."

"So let's drink the night away, fellow madmen. I'm in the mood for some fun. After all, I've been shut away long enough, pretending to be sane. It's quite an effort."

"I know you well," Diego said with his broad smile, "and I don't believe you've ever had a sane moment in your life."

"Nor you," said Carlos, "living in your stinky shack of god-knows-what, in converse with the vilest gods. So, let's have our fun." Carlos made a wide gesture to them, as though he was the royal host and they, the peasants. But, that was only right, he thought, since he was a god granting them audience. He had already noticed how they seemed to worship his beauty, elegance, carelessness and potential for brutality.

Diego stirred the contents of his pan over the altar flame and ladled it into three cups. No one noticed that he gave the larger part of it to Carlos. Taking a long draft, Carlos coughed. "Still the same stinky stuff but what a kick!" He quickly drank again and instantly adapted. His pupils enlarged and blood rapidly flowed to his genitals, giving him a huge hard-on. "It's hotter now, too," he said with a grin and swiftly pulled off his unitard. His naked body was luminous and breath-taking in its wild beauty, and the little man in the corner gasped and gaped.

"It's all part of being a god," Diego said with a laugh. "Since when do they wear any clothes?" The small man tittered and bared his teeth in a grimace of painful desire. What a fool, Carlos thought. Diego watched as Carlos became violently alive. Inevitably, he seized the pan and served himself the remainder.

"It's good, you're right," he said, "but hot. Oh yes! This is powerful stuff. What on earth do you put in it? I'm hallucinating already. This shack is lit up like a cathedral and pulsates like something alive." Carlos shot to his feet and began pacing. The little man's jaw dropped at the beauty and potential for violence of his naked body in movement. "My god," Carlos said, "Holy, holy, holy everything, everyone, even you silly *brujos*. Let's get out of here!"

He strode into the moonlight and threw his arms up in an embrace. The forest was singing and the stars were moving toward him. The two shamans followed him into the moonlit forest. Diego held one of his masks in his hand. Carved with chaotic features that suggested many creatures, it was clearly an image of the Dark God, primitive and frightening. Carlos kept pacing and rubbing his body. "I'm there, friends, there with the gods! They're gliding toward me in a throng of pulsing light, singing. How easy you make it for me."

"Put on your true, sacred face," Diego said. "You must greet the gods properly." He handed the mask to Carlos.

With the mask on, the universe spun in circles to Carlos, filled with brilliant light and color whose patterns and compositions changed constantly, and he was silent, dazzled. He had no sense of its being night at all. He began to shriek in the language of the gods, then grabbed the little man and threw him to the ground. Effortlessly, he tore his pants down and shoved his engorged penis into the little man's anus. The shrieking voices of the gods demanded that this man and all corrupt matter be inseminated by the sacred. Only then would the earth survive. It must feel the agony of the gods and one, only one that the gods would choose, must be killed; sacrificed in the ritual of godhead. The little man's eyes bulged and grew round with shock and pain, but he tried to suppress his cries and keep still. Suddenly, Carlos was off him, scaling the nearest tree, then jumping and swinging through the forest. At last, he was purely mad. There was but one moment of confusion. He was no longer Xochiquetzal, a gentle god, but Tezcatlipoca, the Dark God of violence and perdition. But he was full of ecstasy as well as violence, flying in union with the gods and the cosmos.

He left the two shaman behind. The little man sobbed softly and finally said that he would like to have been warned of the ritual's consequences. He would never have even looked at Carlos if he had known how he would be used. He touched himself gently and winced, pulling his tattered pants back on.

Diego smiled broadly again. They had drunk hardly any of the liquid. Carlos had drunk it all, oblivious to them. "There are a few disadvantages to this ritual; but, you'll be alright soon enough. He's even done that to me, the pig! It's part of his damned godliness. But, a better killer we'll never find. I used to have to hire degenerate thugs to do it, and you never know when one of them will try to kill you, too. I had to shoot and kill three of them. This way, there will be a dead woman by the hot spring before dawn and no more hassles than what you've just experienced. You did say that you wanted to witness a spirit possession. The gods are not congenial and polite. At least, the PRI has given us something we need, and here we're both on the wrong side of the bridge, eh?"

The little man laughed and then touched his wound, wincing again.

Carlos knew nothing of this as he flew through the trees to the sacred spring. He immersed himself in the warm waters as the shrieking voices of the gods demanded; and, when his head came out of the water, he felt the blood coursing to his genitals again and his infinite masculine power heralded by the gods. Like all gods, he would penetrate the world's inert matter and make it live, sacred and holy again. As he rose from the water and put his mask back on, his genitals grew to an enormous size, a vast knife to purify the world. As he stepped lightly back into the forest, he felt his genitals leading him. He could hardly wait for the first thrust of his huge knife. He grabbed a tree brutally, as he would in sex. Walking over moist clay, he suddenly fell to the earth and, finding a good mixture of the yielding and unyielding, thrust his genitals again and again into the ground, covering himself with soil in the process.

Then he scaled a tree and began to fly through the forest. He was Tezcatlipoca now as he flew, his muscles on fire, agony and ecstasy at once. He looked for prey; that was how he thought of the corruption he must enter and render sacred again. It was dark but his eyes were cosmic fire, all-seeing. Again, he felt the endless pain and turbulence of the gods. There was thunder and lightning within him, Tloc and Quetzcoatl, smashing into one another, their muscles wrenching and thrashing, their mouths grimacing in pain, their genitals colossal and fierce. He felt the Dark God Tezcatlipoca, who was nothing but darkness and agony. It was so beautiful, brutal and free to be the Dark God and he shrieked ecstatically in the language of the gods.

As he flew over the forest, he saw a small, impoverished farmhouse, a short distance away. Here was his chance to inseminate and purify with his sacred power. A sheep was loose at the edge of the forest. It looked soft, gentle, and pliant in the moonlight. Here was weakness, corruption that must be filled with sacred strength, the agony of the gods. He leaped in a perfect vertical drop and landed on the lowest branch. The sheep heard and smelled him but could not see. With another leap, he had the sheep, pulling its hind legs over his torso and penetrating its anus again and again. The creature bawled loudly in pain and fear, but Carlos only had one orgasm after another into its helpless body. A weak thing it was, he thought. He threw it aside in disgust and scaled the tree again. There was blood, semen, soil and hair on his genitals. It was now anointed and holy, and it continued to lead him.

The farmer who lived in the small house came out into the moonlight with only his pajama pants on, suspecting the attack of an animal. He counted his sheep and cows and inspected the bawling sheep incredulously, feeling the blood on its hindquarters. He was carrying a gun and stood still, looking into the forest in confusion. Then he moved slowly into the trees with quiet stealth. In a moment, he was directly below Carlos. Carlos smiled and bared his teeth like the gods: he was enjoying his night more and more as Tezcatlipoca. As the man stopped and was still, suspecting the presence of a predator but never imagining that it could be directly above him.

The night was balmy and the wind gentle in its dust of moonlight, the man thought, beautiful to man and beast alike. What am I doing? he thought and lowered his gun, embarrassed at the thought of killing anything. He turned back. Carlos, on the other hand, felt nothing but how engorged his genitals were, how predatory he felt; for Tezcatlipoca loved stalking. In a breath, he leaped down onto the man. He grabbed the gun and threw it into the dark underbrush of the forest where it could not be found until daylight. The man struggled and fought, but he was no match for the god Tezcatlipoca, who very soon had his body in place for intercourse. Carlos slipped between the man's hairy legs and penetrated him again and again. The man cried softly and continued to struggle but did not cry for help. This caused the god Tezcatlipoca to laugh. The man was just like the others; he would never tell anyone that he had been overpowered by a male and raped. He could not even bear to cry for help. The man continued making his soft, pathetic cries that could hardly be distinguished from the wind.

As long as the man struggled, Tezcatlipoca raped him, over and over. Then, the man realized that he must be still to make it stop. And, Tezcatlipoca lost the throbbing of his genitals and stopped. Instantly, he leaped above into the trees and was gone. The man lay, curled on his side, sobbing softly, aware only of the horror, pain and humiliation to which he had been subjected. He would not get up and return to his home for at least an hour. The god knew that; they were all the same, these impotent men who needed his divine brutality. So, the hour belonged to the god Tezcatlipoca for his own pleasure. He walked proudly out of the forest and into the man's small house. He found a woman trying to hide behind a closet door. Instantly, he threw himself against her and covered her mouth with his hand to stifle her screams. She emitted low, stifled cries much like those of her husband.

How silent the world really was, Tezcatlipoca thought, so full of violence and terror, yet never a loud cry for help. Reality was muted; the greatest brutality hardly carried on the wind. Life was multitudes of soft, stifled cries, hardly distinct from the wind, perceptible only to the predator and prey. But then, how could any of them resist him, a god? He ripped the underwear off the woman, threw her to the floor, and raped her again and again with one hand over her mouth and the other arm holding her down. His genitals throbbed with fire while she struggled, then she learned the cosmic law: be silent, without movement, and it will stop. And so it did. He left her on the floor, barely able to cry. At the first loud wail, he was on her again, so she stayed quiet and anguished beyond sound or word. Now his body was covered with dirt, sweat, bits of leaves and twigs, and his genitals were covered with much blood and semen. It could not end there; he knew what the gods demanded. They shrieked their choice of the woman as their sacrifice. He carried the nearly unconscious woman into the forest, slit her throat, and left her beside the hot springs. Diego would find her body and prepare it as the rituals demanded.

Then he quickly scaled the nearest tree and flew to the far side of the forest behind the cemetery. He could see the lights of the town on the peasant's side of the bridge, the faintest glow of so many candles, distant voices of the townsfolk excited over the holiday to come, the life of mere human beings and sanity. This pleased him, and he sat in the trees until the morning light. The chemicals in the mezcal were wearing off, and he was able, in stages, to understand that he was not a violent god, but a man, Carlos Ruiz, who lived in a palace across the bridge. At last, he could swing through the forest and then walk to his home in the early morning light, climb to the roof and enter the attic window that Diego had jimmied for him. He closed it with a thud, turned the lock and smiled.

They would, once again, have no idea how he had gotten out of the house. He went to his room and fell into white bedding that quickly turned black and red, and he let the real world take him as he was. What need had he for concealment, he thought with a smile. Diego had been right; he loved being the Dark God. After sleep, he would remember nothing. Already, it was clouding over, the forest and what he had done there was fading away. Intriguing, being a madman, a man, then so many gods, he thought and lost consciousness.

An hour later, his father was standing over him, feeling horror and disgust. There was his son—indiscriminate murderer and rapist—covered with the soils of his crime and dead to the world. Alvaro sank into a chair, letting it all crystallize in his mind, then he rose and awakened Javier. "It's happened again, *awful!* You *must* come and see it or you won't believe. Come at once!" The two men entered Carlos' bedroom. There was the beautiful body of Carlos, covered with dark soil, leaves, bark and grass. His genitals were covered with blood and semen, and his hands and arms were drenched with blood. Incredibly, his face showed an innocent, gentle smile.

"This animal, this *thing,* is my son!" Alvaro cried. "Look at him! This is how he came back before. I scraped some blood and semen off his penis for a chemist to analyze, and by-god, you know what he does? He rapes men, women, animals, anything, the ground. Look at him! And that blood on his hands and arms is the blood of a woman. That's whom he kills after raping god-knows-what, and those women must be the ones we've heard of, the ones who disappeared. I say, we lock this animal into a sanitarium, just like his mother, but a *room behind bars* for him, that or kill him and say it's a suicide. It *should* be a suicide! If he had one moment of sanity, he *would* kill himself. But he doesn't; he enjoys his life just as it is. I would kill him here with my hands as he sleeps." Alvaro began to sob.

How strangely beautiful he is still, his grandfather Javier thought, a wild, beautiful animal, a legend almost beyond morality; or am I losing my sanity, too?

"Once he was just a crazy young kid," Alvaro continued in a sobbing voice, "saw strange things that weren't there, did nothing about it. He was passive, even. Now this! Since he's been home from the university, we have this murderer, this rapist, the vilest thing I can imagine. My god, I wouldn't have believed it possible if I didn't see it with my own eyes." He began to sob again.

Javier touched his shoulder, clasped Alvaro, his son, tried to comfort him. "We should just wash him, Alvaro. We can't have a servant seeing this. Let's do it now, then take his linen and burn it. Then we'll talk it over and call Dr. Molina. There must be some reason for this radical change. Maybe we can find out, save the boy. He's still a boy, really, your only child, my only grandchild. We don't *know* that it's hopeless. We'll try to get to the bottom of it. Good, now you've stopped crying. Help me with him. We'll wash him in his bathtub and lay him back into clean linen."

No wonder he can't paint, Javier thought, slowly shouldering the burden.


DIEGO WAS ARRANGING the woman's body by the spring. He had prepared her ritually by immersing her in the hot spring's mineral waters. Now he stretched her body on the grass and admired it in the moonlight. It was only a short time since he had seen Carlos, much too soon for rigor mortis to set in. The body was pure white and luminous, its beauty undiminished by death. He took several photos of it as well as samples of blood and semen in her vagina and some locks of her hair, then he unsheathed his knife and carved symbols of the Dark God on her stomach and thighs. Tezcatlipoca would be very pleased with this sacrificial gift.

For more than a year, Diego had been aware of the Dark God's displeasure with women. Now, women were working like men, even leaving their husbands and owning their own businesses. When poverty struck, as it did for most of those he knew, the men were destroyed by it, not the women. They were the survivors, the ones who cared for their children against any odds and kept the family alive. Most of the village men were drunks or addicts, the fools of poverty, dying young. Men were weakening more every year. It must be stopped. All the *brujos* he knew thought so. Women must again fear men and accept their dominance. It was the only way the earth could stay in balance and survive. Balance between opposing forces was the cosmic law. Its violation displeased him, and he was not surprised when the Dark God began whispering the same dissatisfaction to him. At first, he had been afraid when the god asked him to kill. Up to then, he had lived by causing malign influences, the typical province of the dark *brujos* and most lucrative form of magic. But now, he was accustomed to the ritual and even enjoyed it.

After digging the woman's grave, he again admired her on the grass, illuminated so ideally by the moon and, in shamanic terms, as perfectly light as he was dark. Initially, Diego had merely buried the women. But later, his feelings became more complex. Now he undressed himself and lay beside this lovely dead woman, imagining that he was her husband, the one who was feared and adored in equal measure. Then, he kneeled before her, raised her tenderly up to his chest, and felt her weight falling away from him, arms akimbo, her naked waist to his and her back bent nearly double. He swayed her like this in every direction, felt her lack of resistance and the pure submission to his will that it implied. For nearly an hour, he swayed her in this dance that was the essence of the erotic to him, having orgasms against the lips of her vagina all the while. She might have been his wife, after all. The dead weight of her body, her pure submission, whispered this to him. It was something he had never persuaded a woman to do. No woman had ever completely submitted herself to his dominance, nor had any woman wanted him as her husband, leaving only the quick, crude women he could buy. At some point, all women had sensed something in him that appalled them.

Suddenly he burst into tears at the thought of his loss of her, of his loss of all love from women. For a time, he could not stop crying as he held this beloved, perfect woman who did exactly as he wished. He was not, after all, like his friend Carlos, adored by women. He could not hide what he was. He was doing a terrible thing to Carlos, but it was only natural, he thought, that he should hate his friend. Carlos was too fortunate, too admirable, and underneath it all, he was foul and damaged, even worse than Diego. For Diego was not a madman. He lived for simple satisfactions. He had sanity to torment him, too.

He rose and carried the women to her grave, covered her with dirt and then pulled the forest's underbrush over the site so that it looked natural. Then, he looked at his work. The forest was profuse and chaotic; it could absorb anything invisibly. Only the human world was more profuse and chaotic, eventually destroying and hiding all. A good night's work, Diego thought. Now he would bathe in the spring and return to his small house with its prodigious odor, a stink he enjoyed. It was the musk of his manhood and power as a *brujo*.

THE NEXT DAY, Diego drove to the closest large city in his new car, the fruit of what he called a secret successful business venture. Only one other man knew of it. He enjoyed the thought of himself as prosperous and a businessman as well as a *brujo*. When he arrived at the headquarters of the PRI's main opposition party, he parked his car proudly and walked into the building. At first, he startled the woman at the reception desk. He appeared impoverished and dirty, with a strange odor, someone clearly powerless and without utility to the party. He had only to utter one word, "Andrei," to be instantly understood as an asset. He grinned at the startled look of the woman, then the light of uncomfortable recognition.

"In the rear," she said, trying and failing to smile.

"I know," he said with his broad smile. Andrei's office was at the back of the building, a darkened area no one spoke of or entered, a place arousing only discomfort in those who knew of its existence and function. Diego found the small lightless office near the building's exit, a short distance from the trash receptacles. Andrei was alone, as usual; he had no friends, and no one wished to acknowledge him. He looked up at Diego with his wild hair, cavernous eyes that were overly bright, and a face with the intensity and rigidity of one who seemed to have received an insult, as though he had just been slapped. Andrei was a former KGB agent in Russia who had become too violent for his overseers and had fled to Mexico to avoid the fate he commonly administered to others. He supported himself very comfortably by arranging newsworthy accidents and scandals to befall designated people, the PRI elite in this case. Diego smiled, sat down and felt himself at ease; here again was one more damaged than himself. Business with madmen was perhaps a fine salve for his torments, he thought.

"Have you done it again?" Andrei asked.

"Oh, yes, a lovely one," said Diego and produced several photos.

Andrei looked at them. "Pretty," he said as though it were a shame. He rarely implied such sentiments. "And you have proof that Carlos did it?"

"Just as you requested: blood and semen from inside her as well as some of her hair." He handed a small packet to Andrei, who checked it, then scooped it all up and placed it into a file. "He has a lot of fun with them first, thinks he's a god liberating them."

Andrei laughed. "So you do have supernatural powers?"

"Provided you continue to give me the ingredients I need for my mezcal."

"Is that what he thinks it is?"

"It's a hot stinky mess by the time he gets it, full of herbs and roots. But, if it also has what you provide me, it will always do the trick." Andrei smiled and handed him a small packet as well. "I've wondered how you find proof of the murder in what I give you," Diego said.

"It's an American technique involving chemical analysis and DNA. But, that's not your concern. When's the next one?"

"Very soon, the Day of the Dead," Diego said. "The 'old ways' place sacrifices on the fiesta days. Besides, it's my favorite holiday." He smiled broadly again.

"Food for thought," said Andrei with the ghost of a smile. "The dead are so useful. Why not their own holiday?" He kept a light tone between assassins; since, after all, they were predators circling the same prey.

"I also want my payment. This work is tricky and dangerous."

Andrei handed him a huge sum of money in bills small enough to avoid suspicion. Diego spent close to an hour counting them while Andrei again inspected the new file and its photos. "Nice to do business with you," Diego finally said. "When will you spring this on the PRI?"

"Closer to the election," Andrei said. "But don't ask for details. We are silent marauders, you and I, and actually we don't know each other; nor, strictly speaking, do we exist."

"We're shadows, absolutely," Diego said with a laugh, "phantoms, a job that pays so well. You know, my friend, I consider you a *brujo*, too."

"There are some parallels," Andrei said. He kept up the banter since after it lay only conflict and death. "Be sure to leave by the door just behind you."

"Oh yes," said Diego. "After all, I was never here."

"I operate in similar obscurity," said Andrei. "Come again, after your working holiday, the Day of the Dead." He shook hands with Diego, noting that the Mexican was strangely pleased by conventional business gestures. The poor SOB thinks he's nothing but a savage living in a forest, Andrei thought.

When Diego went out the door, the smell of garbage assailed his nostrils, a stark reminder of decay. The light, bantering mood of Andrei vanished and he thought, again, of the terrible thing he was doing to the one man he had ever considered his friend. He remembered when they met and how the bizarre had defined every moment they had spent together, even from the beginning. He recalled it in all of its bittersweet strangeness and beauty. There was once an old abandoned house with windows boarded up, far out in the woods and slowly subsiding into the forest. Children made up horrible, thrilling stories about it, and all were frightened to enter its near-absolute darkness. Diego and Carlos had been children then and of course, both had heard tales of this ominous house.

One night, Diego drank nearly all of his father's tequila and vowed to spend the night there alone, piercing its mystery and proving his pre-adolescent self a kind of superman. He entered the door, egged on by a few children who fled at the first creaking steps he took on its ancient wood floor. He was terrified and ecstatic to be there, exactly where he was forbidden to be. Its darkness seemed to embrace and receive him, as though it understood his need for the forbidden. A few rays of light penetrated the hallway, and he could see a living room moldering away into the forest

Then he heard a sound from the second floor and was paralyzed by terror and joy. Slowly, he ascended the noisily creaking stairs. Then he was on the second floor walking into the hallway. The sound came from a single room. He reflected that anyone there must know of his approach. Every step creaked on the floorboards and echoed against walls eerily alive with dust and the tiny moving bodies and ephemeral gauze of insect and arachnid lives. Then, he was standing in front of the room from which the sound came. It was not a regular sound like the creaking of a door in the wind; it reflected the irregularity and diffusion of consciousness. He opened the door with the broadest of smiles, as though entering the body of a woman for the first time.

He found a beautiful young boy in the room, roughly his age, sitting on the floor, playing a few notes on a primitive flute. "I found this thing here, so I'm welcoming you with it," the boy said in a strangely confident voice, as though he owned the abandoned house. "And, you are welcome to some of this." It was a marijuana cigarette, already lit. "It's even wilder with this. You have no idea how complex shadows are, how intricate the light that is just barely here." The beautiful boy smiled.

Diego felt that he was in a dream. He sat on the floor with the boy and smoked. Then, he saw what the boy meant by the darkness that was not really dark, but composed of shivering particles, wind currents so minute he had never noticed them before, shimmering shadows constantly in flux, perpetually brimming. It was alive, this darkness that so terrified others, and it made him feel as though he no longer possessed himself, but was part of a surging, tantalizing process. He no longer thought that he was in a dream, but in someone's waking fantasy, perhaps this boy's. He laughed at this and was suddenly aware of the many timbres of his own voice.

"I'm Diego," he said, just to hear the same fluid, manifold parts of his voice again.

"I'm Carlos," the boy said. "They're all afraid to come here. What fools!" The boy's eyes were sparkling like water, though there was no light, only this paradoxical darkness more illuminating than light. "Do you know why we're here, together?"

"No," said Diego.

"It's our home," said Carlos, "the real one. It's disintegrating. We're disintegrating."

"Oh, yes," said Diego, now one who lived in twirling particles and pulsing moments of light.

"We're only boys, but already, we're the worst, damned."

Diego only stared. His impulse was to agree, but he started laughing instead, then the two boys both burst out laughing. As soon as Diego could speak, he said, "Well, let's have some fun being damned," and they laughed again. Strangely, his answer echoed throughout their relationship ever after.

Suddenly Diego felt tired. He had hardly slept. He stopped at a cantina and drank whiskey. Instantly, he felt a jolt of energy again. He thought of all the money he had made. This called for a celebration. He deposited most of the money in his bank account, went into an upscale store and bought himself an elegant suit of clothes. Next he rented a hotel room for the night, bought a bottle of whiskey, and took a thorough shower that removed all of his *brujo* odor. He put the clothes on and looked at himself in the mirror. He was nearly handsome with his thick hair brushed carefully back. Now, it was time to buy a woman for the night. He returned to the street and found women who were suddenly receptive. Good, I'm hiding it, he thought.

He brought a dark, voluptuous woman up to his room, turned on the radio for music, and poured her a whiskey. He smiled at her, thinking she could not possibly know that his last lover was a dead woman. "I like to start slow, then I'm a little rough, but I'd never hurt you. Take your clothes off. You're very beautiful, and I want to see you drink and dance naked." To his pleasant surprise, the woman seemed delighted to do as he asked. They danced and she began to remove his clothes as he kissed her and caressed her body with the intent of slowly arousing her. They became playful with this ritual, he trying to excite her gently as she continued to disrobe him.

Ultimately, he enjoyed himself more than he ever had before with a living woman, pretending as he was to be a rich, sophisticated man. The woman was somewhat experimental sexually, but there were clear limits that gave him his typical feeling of dissatisfaction. He could not feel her absolute submission and surrender, as he had with the lovely dead woman, but he became hot, excited, and satiated nonetheless. Well, what of it? he thought. He could be the lover of both the living and the dead, a voyager between worlds, like Carlos, a bit of a god himself.

WHEN CARLOS AWOKE, he was ravenous, wolfing down a huge breakfast; his body felt as though it must have carried out many magical feats of strength the night before, wherever he had been. His father and grandfather had already had a long talk with him, and he was aware that he had undergone another period of madness that was nothing but a blank in his memory. Once again, he was confined to a small area and received increased amounts of medication regularly, with old Antonio watching him swallow it. Later, Dr. Molina would come to see him. When he finished his feast and at last stretched his arms and legs completely, he felt a tremendous strain and pressure in his muscles and joints. What was I doing, he wondered, fucking nonstop all night? He laughed and thought, that's what it feels like. It must have been a hell of a party, whatever it was.

He walked again through the living room in nothing more than his bathrobe. He wanted to exercise in the gymnasium, as he did every morning, but it was out of the question. His body was too pained and exhausted. He sank into a huge welcoming chair and put his feet up. Then, something strange happened: his muscles began to tremble, to move uncontrollably. It continued for a minute or two and ceased. He was appalled: his body had never failed him before. He got up and went to the living room's elaborately framed, immense mirror. His face was pale and his eyes lacked their usual curiosity and life; they looked narrow and predatory. When he saw that deathly look in his eyes, he felt a prickling on the back of his neck. He ran his hand over his face and opened his robe, touching his body everywhere, trying to find its malady. The robe dropped to the floor.

Again, the impossible occurred: in the mirror suddenly was his body transformed into that of the Dark God with a bizarre, chaotic mask-like face. In an instant: this muscular, limitless body had soared through the forest in virtual flight, full of glowing, unearthly light and music sacred in its wildness. It had been gorgeous, reckless, erotic, violent, ecstatic. He heard the shrieking voices of the gods and nearly answered. As suddenly as the vision began, it vanished.

It was a flashback from his period of madness last night, he decided. All he had remembered was going to Diego's cabin and drinking some mezcal. But, the memory must have come from the period that followed. My god, he thought, do these stinking *brujos* really know something? Is there a naked, direct relationship to the universe, a night of gods and their agony, their violent play and excess, and earthly life as well? And, do the gods play with people? Had he done something with people that he might have encountered in the forest? If so, it was beautiful, cosmic, lit up with ecstatic eternity, as this one memory divulged in sacred power to his mind, now.

He sat down again quickly. The vision was a supreme, life-altering experience, but it had taken something from him, too. His face looked haggard, older, and his body was lacking its former agility and strength. He must have this experience again, but not soon. First, he must recover. His madness had never attacked his body before. Was he changing? His world view and that of the gods did assume extreme change, metamorphosis; or rather, this was true of the gods he knew before he came home and drank Diego's mezcal. This other god, who apparently had seized him last night, asked far more of him. Could he endure the god again? But he must: the vision was the most exquisite moment he had ever experienced, a symphony of body, color, light, music, nature, and he was its center.

He looked more carefully at himself in the mirror and saw age and worry on his face. As his hand moved over it, again his fingers displayed convulsions. He felt intense fear, even terror, at the likelihood that he might lose the advantages with which he was born, the double life he had been living until then, the young Adonis and then the Dark God who had lit up his body in flames, a cosmic fire, devouring. Yes, he concluded, a night of this made him five years older, at least. Again, he inspected his body in fear.

Finally, he burst into uncontrollable laughter. What an awful place this world is, he thought. No wonder the gods scorned it, preferred their chaos, their infinite turbulence and agony, creation and destruction as hideous as they were beautiful. So would he scorn this human world, he thought. Oh, yes, so would he! Even if it consumed his mind and body.


IT WAS THE Day of the Dead, and Carlos awoke still exhausted and weak. Dr. Molina had seen him two days before and commented on his physical deterioration, setting up appointments for brain scans and examinations by neurologists. He had taken blood samples to determine Carlos' metabolic function and possible nutritional deficiencies. The change in Carlos shocked him; he had no idea how it could have happened so suddenly, and while his patient had been nowhere but the confines of the Ruiz estate. Carlos only smiled at his bewilderment. You know nothing of gods, physician, he thought. You can heal only the inferior race, man. You will never touch my malady: it is sacred, that of the gods.

He had experienced two more flashbacks of his night as the Dark God, neither having any contact with people. He saw only the intoxication of flying over, through, and within all of nature as the gods did; it was beyond anything he had ever experienced in his previous hallucinations and periods of madness. He denigrated Flower Bird, that pathetically gentle god; but the lesser god had perhaps prepared him for the greater one. Now he wanted only the vast darkness of this god, who was volcanic, a destroyer in explosions of the most violent beauty, anarchy, beyond understanding. The other gods were secondary.

He did not care if it drained his body. If he died, he would only join the Dark God forever. He was the favored one. The god's own shrieking voice had said this in words that flew to him as serpents covered with flowers. They coiled about him, irresistible in their unearthly power. Was he even Carlos anymore after apprehending such words?

These memories, which filled his mind all the time, seemed to pulsate with energy and splendor. They created a rhythm, a pulse of all creation and destruction. He could hear it now and then it merged with Diego's low drumming. He smiled. This was the first time Diego had ever summoned him before nightfall; but then, it was the Day of the Dead, their favorite holiday. With a devious grin on his face, he merely waited for old Antonio to fall asleep in his chair. What a foolish Cereberus the old man was to be guarding one summoned by the Dark God, he thought.

Carlos rushed to the attic, found his unitards and in an instant was moving cautiously over the roof. He looked down at his palace, this house of misery and corruption. How much greater to soar above it! He could feel exhaustion impeding him, yet he desired the god more than life itself. A branch broke as he leaped to the nearest tree, and he was barely able to avoid falling to his death. Yet, he only smiled, dancing between life and death, and his leaps became eloquent, his mind tantalized by this dance of consciousness between opposing forces. He could lose all; he could gain all. It did not matter. There was nothing but the drumming, the pulsation of the universe. Whether he lived or died was irrelevant.

He was brought back to the earth by the strong odor of Diego's cabin and his latest concoction of mezcal. He walked in majestically, magically. "Hello, my stinky friend," he said. Diego looked up at his friend's striding, surprising appearance.

"You remind me of the time we met in the woods when we were children. You were macabre, half-demon, yet so beautiful." He looked more carefully, noticed Carlos' deterioration and felt a touch of guilt. "It's our favorite holiday," Diego said with a soft smile.

"That is true and I'm so glad you didn't invite that little rodent *brujo* along."

"No, no. You scared him away.

"Why?"

"He was the first you made holy."

"I don't remember it. But then, he was too silly to remember. I have had memories of your magnificent god, though, Diego, and my night with him."

Diego looked nervous. "Oh, what memories?"

"Exquisite, flying over the earth, doing anything, worth everything. I see why you worship him. It was pure expansion, knowing everything. He has made his dark mark on me, but my life is irrelevant. He is the greatest god, though he attacks my body. I'm barely able to endure him. I could die anytime." Incredibly, Carlos smiled again.

Diego turned his eyes away in confusion and dismay. "Don't do that. I would miss you, my only friend. Perhaps I can intervene with him to protect you."

"You will never succeed. He is omnipotent and all-knowing. But tell me this: why do you worship him by stinking?" Carlos laughed and Diego smiled broadly. That was the last moment of friendship and brotherhood between them. A ferocious glint suddenly appeared in Carlos' eyes. "Where is your mezcal?" he demanded. "I want it all!" Diego had never seen Carlos look or speak like this before, and he instantly feared for his own safety.

"It's here, of course, just waiting for you. I will serve you immediately." He looked nervously at Carlos and poured a large glass for him. Swiftly Carlos drank it down and seized the whole bottle, drinking it all as fast as he could. Diego quickly grabbed his diablo mask and put it on his face. He wanted Carlos to think he was a god, too; that would protect him. The gods fought but never destroyed one another. They knew their combat was a form of pleasure, nearly erotic. Then Diego could only watch Carlos in fascination as he came alive, the Dark God in human form.

Carlos again rapidly paced back and forth, then uttered a loud, piercing shriek. Diego was terrified. He had no idea what was happening. Carlos ran out to the forest, shrieking, "they're here; they're here! Look at the gods, diablo!"

Diego placed the chaotic mask on Carlos' face. "You must wear your sacred face to be with them." Carlos trembled violently. Diego spoke softly to him, "It is your birthday, the Day of the Dead, Tezcatlipoca. You must appear with mortals and celebrate. It's your favorite day." While he spoke, he pasted photos of the dead women on Carlos' chest and as many as he could on the mask as well.

"It *is* my favorite day," Carlos said. Diego was relieved. He wanted Carlos to frighten women in the fiesta crowds. Carlos shrieked his answer, which again shocked Diego. Then, Carlos raised his fists in joy and shrieked again, mounting the trees and vanishing into the forest. Diego was deeply relieved. It's going out of control, he thought. I don't understand him anymore. Anything could happen now; but then, that is the nature of chaos and the Dark God. At least, he'll terrify women on this day, make them fear for their lives and seek protection from men. That much is certain, he concluded. And, he will kill one for me.

Diego walked back to his cabin, not knowing whether he was pleased or devastated. But then, this was the way of the gods.

They were always beyond comprehension and uncontrollable. He did his best. After this was over and the Dark God was pleased with his work, he would be very glad to return to a simpler *brujo* life. He could not really tolerate direct contact with the gods; but then, that was only human. And Carlos? He would end up dead, that or damaged beyond recognition. He hoped the god would reward them both. The doorway to the gods was perilous, horrifying, and he wanted to open it as rarely as possible. At least, Carlos was now the one beyond the door, in their arms; and he, Diego, could close the door firmly. He did not want to look beyond the door, not at all, not for an instant. Not even a *brujo* is that brave or comfortable with the gods, he thought, and the one he gave them, his friend Carlos? He would end up face down in a ditch, barely alive, if at all. The back of Diego's neck prickled. Perhaps he would soon have enough money to shut the doorway forever. He would far rather be a simple businessman, living in a real house without a *brujo* stench, buying a woman when he needed one. Who knows? One might even love him some day. An easier, simpler life. He dropped into his softest chair, exhausted. Later, he would take a stroll through the cemetery with his diablo mask on, look at the crowds, drink and enjoy himself. The disturbance, dissatisfaction and nostalgia of sanity settled gently into the opposite chair from his, now his only friend in the world.

Carlos was flying through the haunted forest in ecstasy. His strength had returned to him and been augmented, for which he thanked the Dark God. He flew, swung, danced in the trees, god's acrobat; the embodiment, the most vivid reflection of the sacred to this impoverished human world. He had no idea whether it was day or night, summer or winter. His life was the universe pulsating in light, color, joy, beauty, death and horror at once, the eternal celebration and its explosive end. Then he saw the crowds assembled at the cemetery in masks and costumes, some dancing. This was closer to holiness and the gods. It pleased him as it did the Dark God. He would not have to inseminate or kill anyone in these crowds. But their dancing was as nothing compared to the dance of the gods, themselves, creating and destroying the universe. He jumped down from the trees and danced into the cemetery.

This was the cosmic dance, the way the gods created all living things until they begged for destruction and, in holiness and light, pulsation, were destroyed. He danced through the tombstones with this sacred message to human beings. His mind was in eternity as he did so, and he saw and danced all of life, form, creation. It was glistening, thunderous, raw, erotic, enlivening, holy, until it must be destroyed to make way for the new. This dance was the cosmos itself, and he was showing it to human eyes for the first time: their true Eden, their paradise.

The crowds saw him, were hushed. Some came closer to this fountain of holiness, pointing at him. Then, several men began running toward him; he could not allow this. He was above them, exquisite, all of glory: they could never touch him. Humans could only understand the gods and the cosmos from a great distance or as a reflection. They were not made for it, as he was. He flew back into the trees and from the highest tree he shrieked to them in the language of the gods. He enlightened them, told them of the sacred dance they had witnessed, then he disappeared. Humans could not tolerate gods for long; that he knew for certain. So, he haunted the forest and made it light up, splay outward prismatically with color and glowing energy for hours. This was his true purpose, his meaning, the message he brought from the gods to humans and all of nature.

He spent the night in the forest, purely in union with his gods. He saw manifold states of being, universes, one after another. The Mayans had believed in five suns and five earths with more to come, but he saw far beyond this and all in his own imagination, far beyond his history and culture. He was the originator and director of universes, and he threw them into the night sky, the gods' acrobat. Each cosmos began as a single vibrating chord of music, then more chords jumped into being and harmonized with one another. There was a universe of spheres he could touch with his fingers, of a deep, rich golden color with edges of crimson, in which nothing ever paused or stopped. All movement met its goal and became further motion. All questions were answered and replaced by new questions. All communication was instantly understood. Omniscience was achieved by holding a sphere above one's head. All hands reached and met another hand. All was laughter and continuity. He saw the miracle of his poor father, Alvaro, laughing and ecstatic in the never-ending painting that was this sphere of a universe.

There was a universe of cubes—red and green with yellow at the rim where all consciousness was locked into motion at eye level, along lines, all paths speeding on an angle that always turned onto another. Each thing met its opposite with no time to greet, and all creatures cried out in agony like the gods, themselves. Then, Carlos threw a universe of ideas into the forest night sky, as he had the other universes, but this one could only exist for that inferior race, man, and not reflect the divine thought, laughter and play of the gods. Instantly, he replaced it with a universe of flowers, pink accreting to pure crimson, petals upon petals growing into infinity, stamens reaching, delicacy such that nothing harsh or cruel was possible. How dazzling and strange, he thought, that such a thing could even be imagined, how unique a display for his violent gods.

But why not a universe of musical tones, all variations on all themes, a place where nothing was material or concrete, yet all the cosmos was implied, felt, filled with the most breathless, romantic longing; all, all and everything, only to vanish in a tone. But why not a universe of feathers, where all beings were floating from one plume to another, pulling them apart to see further, a horror for philosophers but a delight for writers who wrote their works with giant plumes and heard the incongruous cries of trumpets calling them to greatness. Yet there was also a universe of crystals, where forms were both implicit and real, gently absorbed in their unimaginable growth, never predictable, ever new, metamorphic, metamorphoses again and again.

And, it all turned into a universe of silk, where only serpents lived, madly coiling and uncoiling in the most ecstatic bodily sensation. But, that became a universe of mirrors, in which the slightest event, the fall of a dust mote reflected to infinity, falling in all possible spaces at once and hence never vanishing. And, this became a universe of love—what joy, ecstasy, envy, what scheming and malice—a universe of night and shadows, like the one in which he met Diego.

Carlos laughed in creating what could only arouse the playful laughter of the gods; and so even they could, for a night, forget their agony. All these cosmic states came and went in the forest as he lay on the bough of a tree, creating, directing, dancing. It often seemed that he was dancing them all into being through the trees, supreme intoxication. No man ever saw it, for the inferior race could see so little, a tiny dark corner of misery called existence. And he, he! could create the greatest sound and light show on earth for the gods. They could all see his unique creations, for he was the gods' acrobat. He could originate, let a universe grow or lapse into another, letting it all vanish at last, leaving only the most intense love to mark its passing.

So passed the night for Carlos, but it was all nights, all times. Now I can live forever, he thought, and now I can die, too. In the dawning light, he saw a woman returning from the celebration. She had taken off her mask and was no longer dancing. He heard the Dark God shriek that she must be the sacrifice. He tore his clothing off to purify himself and then dropped down, raped and killed her, leaving her body beside the spring. He returned to the trees for another afternoon and night, raced and flew like the gods, in love with eternity, until he felt the presence of the dawn, the most beautiful fountain the gods had ever created and he saw it, mesmerized, its prism of colors opening with ecstasy like a women's sex, like a god's palm. He was silent, dumb with love, for many hours, until his thoughts seemed to change strangely. He could see the time of day: afternoon. He touched his body in the trees and became aware of his sexual force. He copulated against the tree trunk and then hung on a branch, covered with what he could now see as blood and semen on his genitals and blood covering his arms. He was blind to his body before this moment. He stood on the branch and suddenly he knew he was not a god but a man, Carlos. Carlos, Carlos Ruiz, he said in wonder, who lived in a labyrinthine palace of error and torment. Then the god took him again and he was bathed in radiant light; he smoldered, thundered, was all and everything until again, the inconceivable: the god left him and he found himself in a tree, in a forest, a particular place and time and then, the fact, a man, a man named Carlos.

He saw a woman, quite old, close to the spring. Instantly, he was afraid that she would find the body but no, it was gone. Diego had already buried it. Diego . . . that was a man he had known for many years, a repellent, cunning man who stank and was abhorrent to everyone. Now he shifted between man and god until he grew dizzy, faint. He knew that he must follow the old woman. She could not be close to the spring, for it was holy. He heard the god shriek for her death, which he must fulfill. But, exhaustion overtook him. He ran after her but she somehow got away. He would have killed her, but he could not stay a god long enough. He was an exhausted man, a failure.

He saw her from the trees, being welcomed by another white-haired woman and a group of young girls. They were all getting into an automobile. But this must not be allowed. They had been claimed by the god, but he, Carlos, had been too weak to kill them. He stepped out from the highest tree into the light and wind and shrieked the Dark God's curse upon them. The god said he would find them all and kill them. It was cosmic law and could not be broken. Then, exhausted, he moved back into the forest and fell, breaking branches to stop the impact of his fall, and lying still on the forest floor, a man, Carlos, a man again, exhausted beyond anything he had ever known.

He had lost it all. He was so weak he could barely stand and walk home and, with his last bit of strength, leap up to the attic and enter his house. Unsteadily, he walked down the stairs and entered his bedroom, falling at last into bed. Then there were shouts all around him. The house was in a pandemonium. "He's here! He's here!" he heard all around him. Through eyes half-closed, he could see old Antonio talking excitedly to his father, then he lost consciousness.

Alvaro cried, "How did he get back in? He has been gone two days, and now he just appears! But look at him: blood and semen! And my god, he looks ten years older. Look at the blood; he has killed again. I can understand nothing of this! What is happening?" He burst into sobs and fell into a chair.

Javier and Dr. Molina scrutinized Carlos more carefully. "Well, what do you think?" Javier asked Dr. Molina, his voice controlled with great discipline, only slightly unsteady.

"My poor, dear friends," Dr. Molina said. "We haven't seen the forest for the trees. The blood and semen on his body are not the key. This boy has been drugged and with truly awful toxins." He took Carlos' blood in three large syringes. "I can now assure you that I'll find out what has changed him. This may not entirely be the result of his madness at all. I will test him for a great range of illegal chemicals, and I'll speed the process so that we know by tomorrow. Someone has drugged him, and this blood will tell the whole story." Dr. Molina touched Javier's shoulder and then Alvaro's. "Don't despair, my friends. I'm convinced we now have the truth. When he awakens, try to find out how he leaves the house and returns. Someone from outside, someone unspeakably evil, has drugged him and we will need to find out who that is and why."

He left them. Javier, too, now collapsed into a chair in front of his bloody, naked, unconscious grandson. The two men were both still in shock, though deeply relieved, silent together and touching one another's shoulders. "Dr. Molina will find a cure," Javier said at last.

"Good," said Alvaro, more exhausted than he had ever been. "I was going to strangle him, and I don't want two murderers in this house." Ah, this house! thought Javier. We live in a palace and a hell of misery and want worse than anything over the bridge. We are more pathetic than beggars.


IN THE MORNING, Javier awoke with a feeling of strength. The whole house had been in shock for two days as they waited for Carlos to return, but now, they would know very soon, Javier told himself as he quickly dressed. He drank a glass of milk and two cups of coffee and hurried out. He had to introduce the new PRI candidate to another audience, a much larger one in the next city. He drove past the speed limit and arrived just in time. I must stay focused, he told himself. There is a mass-murderer beneath my roof, but the world must go on.

When he arrived backstage, he was told that he had just missed an emergency call from Dr. Molina.

Instantly, he began to sweat and tremble. With great difficulty, he steadied himself. It's not for nothing that I am the most powerful man in the state, he thought. He dialed Molina's number and found him there, waiting. "What is it?" he asked.

"A terrible cocktail of drugs in huge concentrations. He's only alive because he's young and strong. There's STP, the most powerful hallucinogen, methamphetamine and alcohol, all in concentrations I've never seen before. The hallucinogen would normally last for days, but the methamphetamine has burned it all at once. Also, there are many herbal substances whose effects are unknown. That is not important. What is important is that this cocktail was given to a paranoid schizophrenic. The result is unimaginably violent behavior and a grave deterioration of his mental and physical condition. This is why he has aged after each administration. You must find out who has been giving this to him. It's clearly no one in your house. It must be someone in the community, and that person is responsible for these murders and for the devastation of your grandson's mind and body. You must act quickly or it will kill him—that or turn him into a doddering idiot. You must find out, Javier! Use all your political power. You must save your grandson and stop these awful murders!"

Javier put the telephone down and fell into a chair as an aide came to him. "The candidate is here now, Mr. Ruiz. It's time for you to introduce him." Javier heard the sounds of the crowd and the music for the first time, though they had been there all the while.

"No," he said. "Have the mayor introduce him. I must return to my family immediately." He walked quickly away and out of the building to his car. The aide watched him in astonishment. He had never known Javier to abandon the party for anything.

# part Three

the survivor

"NOW THIS IS worth seeing," Lynne Lonidier said.

She was standing beside Red and Jean in early December, looking at the town's Christmas decorations. All three women were struck by how humble the scene was yet how diligently created. Four streets of the town were completely covered with white paper streamers. The white flower-like paper constructions were attached to strings and then to ropes that hung from the tops of buildings on both sides of each street, creating a flying white ceiling over the entire area. Similar ropes with white paper flowers, doves and other religious or folkloric figures hung from the sides of buildings. In the wind, they created a wildly moving city of delicate white, like fleece or the feathers of birds or imaginary angels, casting equally riotous shadows: a primitive holy city or a bit of heaven, with white and dark spiraling together.

I have no religion, yet I almost expect to hear the whispering of angels, Jean thought. So simple, humble, yet implying so much hope and good will in the face of poverty. So Indian, Red thought, a flying holy city that dances between white and dark. Good and evil are never absolutes to them; they fly or float together, then separate, like the streamers. "I can see why you love it here," Lynne said. She had been invited to stay with Red and Jean for the Christmas fiestas, which lasted nearly a month, from the Feast of the Virgin of Guadalupe on December 12 to the Epiphany Feast and Three Kings celebration on January 6. A time for so much life, Lynne thought, yet they say it will be a time of death, too. In different words, they all thought, it is good that we are here together, a time when everything has meaning, secrets dark or light; and just possibly, barely, we might catch a breath of truth. We are those who know enough to watch and wait.

They strolled through the streets beneath the white paper streamers. On one street corner, a photographer had set up his shop: a huge painting of an elegant city of many churches and in front of it a life-sized white wooden horse with a decorative saddle. He also had several beautifully woven tunics beside him. His business was thriving: both adults and children wanted to be photographed on the back of a white horse or standing beside it while wearing a festive tunic, as though entering or riding out of a wealthy holy city. "St. Peters and the Vatican on a white horse," Red said. "Is anyone up for it? A senior can maybe just barely get up on that horse without the whole thing falling over." They laughed and continued walking.

There were several vendors on every street corner, Indian families of children with curious, ardent eyes and women with tired but determined faces, watching their wares. Some sold chains of flowers that were used to decorate statues of saints at home or in the churches. Others sold vegetables like moss and cacti that were bought as background to nativity scenes. One woman and her four wild children were selling, paradoxically, white paper doves attached on strings to be used as garlands. Others sold ribbons, small glass figurines for nativity scenes, brilliantly colorful toys—rubber balls and drums with drumsticks, dolls and trains, tiny plastic babies and trucks, papier-mâché men and women on donkeys. All could be bought for a few pesos and delight a child at Christmas. A poor man's Christmas has never lacked color, Lynne thought.

"Shall we stop for a beer?" she asked.

"We expect nothing less from you," said Red. "We know a poet's religion."

"The best beer is over the bridge, of course," Jean said. "It's a different world."

"I want a beer in both worlds," Lynne said with a smile. They came upon the outdoor stand of a beer vendor, placed next to a crumbling wall. Six chairs were placed around him, and mariachi music blared from a big radio.

"This is the way it's done on this side," Red said," under the sky. The first round is on me." The three women sat together and sipped beer from their bottles. The stand was within the area of paper streamers, and they continued to watch the white city fly around them.

"I take it back," Lynne said. "I only want to drink here. I love the wind blowing through all the white stuff."

"It does have a spiritual ambience," Red said, "a wild and rugged one."

"That's the only one I'm interested in," Lynne said, "and you know the poet's religion." They smiled and stared at the crowds. "But what on earth does this have to do with murdered women?"

"Ah, that," Jean said. "We don't know, or rather, we know too much. There are too many possibilities. They happen during the fiestas, so something will happen during your stay. What do you think?"

"Only the kind of thing I read about in the American newspapers. A very rough summary would go something like this: Mexico is changing. Women are getting jobs, many in the *zonas internationales* around the border towns. The power balance between men and women is affected, and the definition of the family is changing. One of the border towns, Ciudad Juarez, has seen many murders of women, mostly young women with jobs. There are rumors—devil worship, a wealthy family preventing the police from working on it, horrible stuff and no end in sight. But, you live down here. You must know all about it." Her response was greeted by complete silence that lasted too long.

"You *do* know about that?" Lynne asked again.

There was more silence, finally broken by Red. "No, we didn't know that." She looked at Jean.

"We've more or less been living like Indians," Jean said. "The 'big picture' is for the developed world. We're *really* here now."

Lynne's eyes were bright with fascination and consternation. "Well, the next round is on me. I'll get them, then you tell me what the hell you mean by that!"


ANDREI HAD NEARLY finished his work for the day. He checked his files again and packed his briefcase. He'd given three more doses of drugs to Diego so he could arrange killings during the holy month. His work was nearly done. He felt some satisfaction in that. Yes, an assassin has the pride of his work, too, he thought. He looked up at the other workers, all avoiding him. Sheep, he thought. A few changed facts and they could be his prey. He wondered if he was starting to look like an assassin. Probably not, he thought. Even that savage, Diego, looked normal in a business suit.

With agility, he ducked out the rear exit. Always the invisible feline, he thought. He walked ten paces, then two bullets from an assault rifle ripped through his head. He fell, dead before he reached the street, his blood spraying all over the pavement.

Instantly, men in ski masks with assault rifles entered the exit. They grabbed all of Andrei's files, computers and the contents of his desk; then disappeared, roaring away in a black SUV.

The stunned employees watched what had happened, then the office manager, a man in his forties with wet, dark hair, a profuse mustache, and the crude features, sagging eyelids and haggard skin of perpetual self-repression, walked in front of them and shouted, "Everyone back to work! Nothing happened! You saw nothing!" The rattled workers looked quickly back at their computer screens. The office manager returned to his office and closed the door. He took out a pocket mirror and thought, I look like an idiot.

In a few minutes, one older woman came into his office. She was dark-haired and heavy-set, with soft arms and a face that was open and lovely despite its age, marking her for family and children. "My god, what are you doing?" she said. "There was a man working there for months, and they killed him. His blood is everywhere, even on the walls of the building outside."

"Not on the building," the office manager said quickly and looked nervous. "We'll get it off the building."

"But someone killed him and took his files. It's . . ."

He swiftly rose and interrupted her. "You are becoming too old to be working in Mexico. What are you, some grandmother? If you want to keep your job, you will never say any of that again to anyone, not even your family. Especially not your family, or you will all be in danger. Everyone else knows how to behave here. You'll never hear a word about it from any of them. Nothing happened. No one was here. No one was killed. Understand?"

The woman breathed, "Mother of God . . ." and walked back to her desk. The rest of the staff stayed an extra half-hour in hopes the body would be removed by the time they left, and they would not have to think of it again. From time to time, they stared back at the empty desk and chair in the rear. It was, after all, now safe to do so, since No One would ever be coming back.

At the police station, no one claimed Andrei's body within the requisite number of days, and it was dumped into a hazardous waste landfill.

IN BROAD DAYLIGHT, men in business suits brought the files, computers and other materials into Javier's office. The operation leader, a short, stocky Indian with full lips and black eyes with a wavering light that suggested both excitement and uneasiness, stood in front of Javier's desk. "Do you want us to dispose of it?"

"Yes," said Javier. "I'll check what's here, then I want it all at the bottom of the Gulf. Is that animal dead?"

"Oh, yes!" said the leader, suddenly smiling and gentle. "Two bullets straight through the head."

"Good work. And Diego?"

"We haven't found him yet. He has abandoned his shack and all his . . . filth, paraphernalia."

"Where do you think he is?"

He's a *brujo*, thought the operation leader. He can vanish. He can blind your eyes if he wants to. He can be in heaven or hell. "We're working on it," he said, the uneasy, excited look back in his eyes.

"What do the *brujos* say?"

"They say, follow your nose." The Indian smiled.

"Keep it up. He's your top priority. When you find him, bring me his ugly, damned head. I want to bury it myself, feel some of his rotten blood on my hands. Dispose of the rest of him with the files, far out into the Gulf, so nothing ever reaches the shore."

The group of men nodded their assent and promptly left. The operation leader suddenly looked like a man possessed by a passion. He had always wanted to kill a *brujo*. Now he could cut a *brujo*'s head off, too, and see what awful things might jump out. In general, he hated his brutal work, but there were times when, he felt, as now, a certain satisfaction and even pride in it.

We're halfway there, Carlos, Javier thought with pleasure. One monster down, one to go. He had always been proud of his work.


DIEGO AWOKE, SWEATING in his new house in a nearby town. It was the dark time, the pit, about three a.m. He had changed his name and left everything behind. He now always wore business suits and brushed his hair back. He had real pajamas on, like a *gringo*. Still, he could feel the heat moving in. He remembered the last time he went to see Andrei. The woman at the front desk said only, "No one named Andrei has ever worked here. You are mistaken."

Damned! he thought. So they killed Andrei and with it the money he still needed for a new life. Damn it all! He'd stay a stinking *brujo* somewhere else when his money ran out. Still, the Dark God would be satisfied. He had the drugs for three more murders. The last one would be those *gringas*. He had heard rumors that they sheltered frightened women in their house. He would put an end to that. They were still paying workers, but after the house was finished, he would finish them off, too. The Dark God would leave him alone after that. He could close the cosmic doorway once and for all. Flesh could barely stay alive in even the breath of his violent gods.

But damn, they were moving in on him; he could feel it. He wondered with great bitterness whether he would live any longer than Carlos. It was now just as likely that he himself would end up face-down dead in a ditch. Damn them! He did not dare to curse the god, only his servants, who were legion. Incipient sleep began to change his thoughts: danger, red light, red light, danger, dark, oh so dark, he thought chaotically as he dropped back to sleep, dreaming of escape and demons floating after him. He continued to sweat.

CARLOS WAS ENJOYING himself at a lavish PRI fundraiser in his palatial home. He had put some weight on, pure muscle, since he continued to work out in his gymnasium every day. He was strong again, healthy, and looked only a bit older, which had even increased his attractiveness to women. He could have anyone he wanted; they all looked at him sauntering about in his male luxury, power and freedom. His flashbacks were fading, and he was beginning to enjoy even a bit of sanity. Up to a point, of course, he thought with a smile. He would never forget the Dark God's glittering, intoxicating world where he was a powerful god himself and could create his own universe, then a handful of them to toss into the radiance of eternity. No man could forget that kind of power.

But, Diego had not contacted him again, and now it was nearly the holy month. I can fuck a different woman every night if I want to, he thought with a laugh. There's holiness for you. A beautiful girl had been following him around all night, and he suddenly swung around to face her, smiling with his arms partly open. I've got you, his pose seemed to say. She was a blond, wild-haired like a little lion, and green-eyed. How had these genes come to Mexico, he wondered. But then, she had probably tinted her hair blond. It would look better natural, dark and ferocious, Carlos thought, but she was attractive enough for a night. She was wealthy, too, the daughter of a PRI senator. Are the rich better in bed? he wondered. No, probably not.

"Carlos," she said. "I'm Elena. We had a college course together, but you don't remember me."

"But I do," said Carlos, kissing her three times on her cheeks, like a European. "Can I get you another drink, Elena?"

"Actually, I'd love a ride in your car, if you don't mind. I saw it on the way in. It's awfully hot here. It would be nice to get away."

"My pleasure," Carlos said with a smile. Ready to fuck already, he thought. I like it well enough in a car. "Where is your coat, Elena?"

"I didn't bring one."

"So, let's leave our comrades to the heat of their ambition."

They drove away in Carlos' midnight blue convertible. Old Antonio immediately noticed and told Javier. Thoughts suddenly passed at lightning speed through Javier's mind. Well, of course, it's only normal . . . but then, he has killed women . . . he has killed! But he's all right now . . . isn't he? . . . but . . . He told Antonio to immediately find his three bodyguards and send them after Carlos to bring him back. The girl, too.

Carlos and Elena were speeding along the highway to the coast. The moon was crescent, but the light was playing an intricate game between shadowy forests and suddenly luminous fields of grass. "Would you like to go to the beach?" he asked. "A night swim? See the sunrise?" Fuck at every change in the light, he thought.

"That sounds wonderful, but maybe we could find a place closer. Just somewhere in the forest. We can talk."

"Oh, yes," Carlos said. "That course. It was anthropology, wasn't it?" She's in estrus, he thought, can't even wait for the coast. Well, that's fine with me.

"Yes. Then you do remember."

"Oh yes. You've become more beautiful. I didn't recognize you at first."

At that moment, a large black limousine appeared behind them. Damn, Carlos thought, the heat's following me everywhere. He speeded up, then took a quick right into the forest. The car speeded past, its driver looking for an opportunity to turn around. Carlos abruptly drove off the highway and hid the car behind a copse of trees. "You *are* a fast worker," the girl said with a laugh.

"There's a pathway through the forest just beyond." They vanished into the foliage as the limousine passed them.

"Are we being followed?" Elena asked.

"Yes, we might be," Carlos said with a smile. "My grandfather worries a lot during an election."

"I think you can protect me against anything. You're in better shape than those bodyguards." She had spoken directly of his body, and the blood instantly flowed to his genitals. Suddenly, he had a flashback. The forest, the night, the shrieks of gods, the screams of women, the sounds, the sounds of things beautiful and terrible! It all whirled about him—flying like a god, being a god, being anything and everything, his mouth open in wonder . . . They were now on the pathway and he stopped in his tracks, looking at the girl ardently, his hard-on visible in his pants. He could slit her throat, couldn't he? Hadn't he done that? Many times!

Elena saw his excitement and kissed him, pressing against his erection. His hands laced her throat. He could strangle her, too. Anything could happen in the enchanted forest. It was his forest; he shared it only with the gods. Women were interlopers, though so desirable, inevitable.

He heard a sound behind him. Three stocky, breathless men, the security guards for his grandfather, walked onto the path. "Just come with us, Carlos," they said softly. "Javier told us to bring you both home. It's always dangerous during an election.

"Oh, what nonsense!" Carlos shouted. But he immediately acquiesced, frightened by his own thoughts. He took the girl's elbow and walked toward them.

What on earth is this? Elena thought. Who's afraid of the dark?

LYNNE LONIDIER WAS sitting in the house that was nearly completed, her feet up on a soft footrest, a rich, creamy, dark Mexican beer in her hand. As good as it gets in my poet's playground, she thought. It was early evening, and the house was full of noise: innumerable Mexican women were drinking and talking throughout the living room. All had lived in Red and Jean's house for various periods, then returned to their homes again. It was the feast day of the Virgin of Guadelupe, and they had returned for a few hours to celebrate, see one another and meet the *gringa* guest. It's a feminist holiday here and now, Lynne thought, and the secret is that it always was. She knew the story of the dark skinned virgin who appeared one day to a village boy and proved her identity by creating supernatural flowers.

Had Red and Jean really protected all these women? What an amazing thing! Lynne thought. They were quiet librarians for decades in San Francisco, then they came down here and became Mexican revolutionaries overnight without a second thought. That's the unsung wisdom to be found in world travel: the unimaginable flowers into a bold and brilliant truth, right before your eyes. All of the language spoken around her was rapid Spanish, which she could barely follow, and yet she marveled at the scene.

Three young girls were running around the room, playing and laughing. Two suddenly sat down, breathing deeply, and the third approached Lynne rather grandly. "I know that you are a bullfighter," Clara said proudly to Lynne, her dark eyes luminous. "One always recognizes another." Lynne looked up and suddenly noticed the interest shown in this by a tall, regal woman who was watching and listening. Her mother, Lynne thought, also noticing that Red was following the interaction with a bemused expression. You're the creative one, she seemed to be saying. Let's see how you get out of this.

"Well, only part-time or as an adjunct," Lynne said in her imperfect Spanish. Clara clearly demanded a serious answer. "I'm a poet the rest of the time."

"I knew it!" Clara said with a great smile and eyes that were suddenly on fire. "So you know all about the bullfighters of the great *El Norte*."

Tread carefully, Lynne thought. "Well, a bit, of course," she said.

"Then you know if you have to kill the bull. I don't want to. I want to wave the cape, tire him out, and then pet him for my grand finale. But, I don't know if anyone will want to come and see me. Do you kill the bull?"

"Oh, no!" Lynne said emphatically, "I wave the cape, tire him out, and then give him a pop tart."

*"What is that?"* Clara boomed her question as though the universe would stop if she did not know what a pop tart was.

Lynne looked up rapidly. This was perhaps becoming dangerous. Red looked even more amused, and Clara's mother had a stern look on her face that clearly said, You will not get out of this with irony. You will disabuse my daughter of her bullfighter fantasy and you will do. it. right. now.

"Well you see," Lynne began quietly, "it's pastry."

"I knew it! I knew!" Clara shouted in joy. "You don't have to kill the bull! You can just give him a pet or a treat." Clara's mother, Josefina, had since moved to the chair beside Lynne and looked at her even more darkly. Red began to laugh, but softly.

"That's the problem, of course," Lynne said. "Then, all the children of the great *El Norte* want to eat the same kind of pop tart, and it causes tooth decay. So, that's why I just fight bulls part-time. There really aren't many bullfighters in *El Norte* because of that. Many girls who don't make it as bullfighters become pilots of airplanes. Have you ever thought of doing that? There are flight schools to teach you, and piloting a big plane is as courageous as waving a cape before a bull." I seem to be drowning in my own bullshit, Lynne thought and looked directly at Josefina.

"I know only one girl who's flown on a plane, and she threw up. I hate to throw up."

"That only happens the first time. Then you get your wing legs and it never happens again."

"Well . . . I could think about it," Clara said.

"Oh, just imagine it. You're flying through the night in the rain at the top of the world, and every life on board depends on you. How does that sound?"

"It is a great thing. It must be. I want to be great, whatever I do."

"Well, then, you should be a pilot instead of a bullfighter; who after all, only causes children to suffer more tooth decay," Lynne said. Red smiled broadly, as though to say, well done, poet.

"I will think about flying through the night with all those people."

"And you wear a wonderful cap and suit that makes you look like a general."

"Oh!" Clara said and closed her eyes in pure pleasure, as though she had just eaten chocolate. Then, she ran off with the other two girls. Josefina nodded her head slightly in respect to Lynne and smiled as though to say, well done, poet of *El Norte*.

I will never use the word, *mamacita,* again as long as I live, Lynne thought.

IT WAS NEARLY nine p.m., and Javier and Alvaro were walking slowly over the palace lawn in the twilight. Old Antonio had already fallen asleep in his chair. They had privately celebrated the Feast of the Virgin of Guadelupe with wine and a huge meal and were feeling very relaxed. They did not even notice that Carlos was not in the house.

"Do you remember him, then?" Javier asked.

"Just a bit. He was only a boy then. I knew his name, Diego, and that he was very strange. Somehow, he could always get into the house at any hour, picked locks and so on. If we found him, Carlos always defended him, said he had asked him in, though it didn't seem to be true. He was poor, obviously, dirty and oddly smelly. He might have had a father who was a *brujo*. He dabbled in it even then. What on earth could he have had in common with Carlos? Yet, he was always around. They whispered a lot, had secrets, but there was definitely a bond, early, from the beginning. I can't even remember talking to him. He was some kind of vermin we allowed to live, like an odd animal pet of Carlos'. I should have thought more about it. He must have been taking advantage of Carlos' madness all along. I should have known he was trouble and put a stop to it. What will you do when you find him?"

"He will die like a pig, just as he deserves," Javier said. His head will be carried on a bier like a feast day, he thought. I will bury it myself on my own lawn and walk over it. Javier would never say a word of this to Alvaro. Violence is a lonely business, he thought.

Their conversation shifted to Alvaro's painting. "I feel some optimism," Alvaro said. "Carlos has recovered remarkably, and we may be out of the woods. One morning, I painted this canvas. The image just came to me, like the old days, and I worked ten hours straight."

Javier looked carefully at the painting, trying to discern his son's mental state. It showed a woman in the robes of the Virgin Mary, her face brown and strong, out in the fields doing manual labor. Her face was powerful and riveting. The colors were that of the earth and light—ochre, umber, dark green, blue, touches of cinnabar, and her face rose out of it like a natural force. "When did you think of this?" Javier asked, relaxing and appreciating it as art.

"It was just a woman I saw at your first fund-raiser for the new candidate, a peasant woman from the other side. Her face troubled me; it looked stricken and exhausted, then I truly saw it. It was full of amazing strength, the strength to withstand anything. She was suddenly the most important thing in the world; I had to paint her. I can't explain it."

"Never explain, just paint more," Javier said with a smile. He was very pleased to see another recovery under his troubled roof. It was a fine feast day, he reflected, something to really celebrate. He had always loved the story of the Virgin of Guadelupe, and perhaps she had produced another miracle.

IT WAS PAST midnight, and Carlos was celebrating the feast day of the Virgin of Guadelupe in the gymnastics of copulation with Elena. He had sneaked into her father's estate and just appeared in her bedroom in his grey unitard with a big smile and a bottle of wine. Elena laughed at his unexpected appearance and unconsciously opened her robe. She drank a glass, then another, her eyes hungrily following the muscular contours of his body in the unitard. She had never seen a man wearing one, and it seemed perfect for a body as beautifully sculpted as his. Carlos drank a glass, too, then surprised her again by simply jumping on top of her, leaping from his chair to her sofa in a bound. She was breathless as he did this and then tore his unitard and her nightgown off in a few skilled motions. He's perfect, she thought, some kind of god.

They had hardly exchanged words, yet they spent the next three hours in the most strenuous sexual intercourse Elena had ever experienced. She felt as though she was losing her mind, and merely whispered, "You're gorgeous. I've wanted you forever. My god, my god!" Carlos merely bellowed and continued arranging and re-arranging her in several positions of the Kama Sutra and whatever else came to mind. He had discovered that replaying the images of his nights with the Dark God could keep him erect for hours. If this is holy month, I'm a religious fanatic, he thought. This is definitely the only part of sanity worth preserving. He was so much stronger that he could do anything with her. She had no strength at all in his hands. He picked her up, entered her vagina, and partially dropped her out of her window, then had a long orgasm as he held her, something he had once seen in a movie but had improved upon with his strength. Her legs over his shoulders, she was completely dependent on him for life, yet she had one breathless orgasm after another. With a devious grin, he imagined her father outside, seeing this outrageous deflowering of his daughter.

He pulled her back into the room and said with a smile, "Fight me. Try to get away. Try as hard as you can." Elena wrenched herself in one direction, then another, but his strength so overpowered hers that he just bent her exquisitely into a new sexual position and filled her vagina again, to her even greater delight. He laughed. "Why don't you cry for help?"

"Thank god, we're . . . in the unoccupied wing of the house." It was hard for her to talk through passion. "This is . . . the fuck of a lifetime. I'll remember it . . . when I'm ninety." They both laughed, but not for long. He completely flipped her over and entered her vagina from the rear. She began babbling again, "Oh yes, oh yes. Do it again. Oh, yes, keep it up.'

Ah, women, he thought. They say the same thing over and over and how he loved this breathless, limited vocabulary of love. He wanted them speechless, senseless in the head but never the body.

Suddenly he asked, "Do you want me for my money?"

"Oh no, baby, just . . ."

"For my family's power?"

"No, oh just . . ."

"Marriage and children?"

"Just, just . . ."

"Just?"

"Just keep fucking. I just want you to fuck me."

"Good girl." Suddenly they both passed out, then woke up with his penis deep inside her and her legs around his neck. "Isn't it some sort of holiday?" he asked.

"Yes, the Feast of the Virgin of Guadelupe." This struck them as ridiculously incongruous, and they laughed uncontrollably. "Well, the feast part is right," she finally said.


DIEGO FELT VERY alone in a cheap, dark bar, so drunk he could not even buy himself a woman. He could barely stand. His great dark, sweaty head rose and he stared at a blurry bit of red neon light and dark corners, swarming with life like a jungle, of the filthy room in which he stood, where a woman was being fucked against a wall by two men. These places must just grow out of the sewer, he thought. I can't get drunk enough to stop the fear. Well, if they want to kill me, they have to come into this piss-pot of a bar. You want me, you're going to get your prissy pants dirty. You want me, it's going to stink. It was two a.m., so he could leave. He stumbled along in the dark, wet streets, almost oblivious of anything. Almost. Somehow, he registered every shadow that flickered about him.

He lurched into his house and fell on the floor, then crawled around until he was sure it was empty. Strange, he thought. I kind of like this. Live in a crawl space like a spider. Safe, they won't find me. He stood up and dropped into bed, struggling out of his clothes, then lying back.

Always, he thought, always the hour like a pit you fall into, named for the wolf, just before first light. My only friend is the hour of the wolf; my last friend, a crazy Russian assassin who so deserved his stinking death that no one could even pity him. I can't even talk to the *brujos*. Anyone can be bought to give my whereabouts. He could only hide in plain sight, utterly alone, drawing no attention to himself, in a business suit that was growing crumpled, dirty and pungent. Soon it would no longer hide him.

Hot tears seared his eyes and he grimaced. He kicked his pants off and began to masturbate. Isn't it some holiday? he thought. When the semen ran down his hands, he thought, there's one for that whore of a virgin, whoever she was. It was dark, so dark. How he liked that. If he could only live in a dark world, three a.m. and the wolf forever; they'd never find him. No one could stand to come there for him. What impotent self-pity, he thought in further disgust; but no mind, it's better than that gun barrel down my throat.

He kept on masturbating. It was better than drunkenness at dispelling his fear. This damned prick is the only part of me worth anything, he thought. The only truth in this world is this darkness, where bodies are always moving, moving in sex, terror or death, the unholy trinity, he thought. Maybe next time, I'll drink some mezcal myself and blow my brains out for some damned shit of a god. A drink or a throbbing prick are the only things worth living for and even these, only in darkness. Can I ever get away from those assassins? Probably not—end up in

a ditch. Then let my hand be on my prick and let me go out
fucking the damned dark . . .

He slept for a few hours, then woke up sober in the awful
sun, electrified with terror.


LYNNE, RED AND Jean were standing in front of the
small village church on Christmas Eve. They were awed by the
garlands of white flowers and religious symbols hanging by
strings and ropes from the exterior building columns, blowing
in the wind before the facade, the humblest devotion breathing
from every one. Nearly all were made solely of paper, and they
hung in six layers over the center of the church from ropes at
both sides, then another six lines hung directly down from the
center of the last layer, forming a geometric pattern. It's like a
peasant tunic, but one for the whole church, Lynne thought. She
had seen tunics in the same pattern throughout Asia and Africa
as well as the Americas. The church is a peasant in its holiday
best, she thought. The Spirit reflects human beings and what
is best in them: that is the spiritual message to the world and
its reason for celebration. Its essence is human love, altruism,
gentleness, careful work, care of others, and remembrance of the
dead. This word from god or gods is primordial and to know
it is to be blessed. Yes, Lynne concluded, this is a message that
must be remembered ritually each year, lest it be forgotten. The
three women were followers of no formal religion, but they were
among those intrinsically blessed by a boundless sensitivity to
the human world and nature, an appreciation that grew richer
as time passed. To truly see is to praise, celebrate and bless: this
they knew instinctively.

They walked into the church's interior and were met by
even more paper decorations. Colored paper streamers joined
the entire structure of the building to the ceiling and altar,

creating a cosmic circle in the church's interior. There were more paper garlands hanging from the ceiling in myriad shapes: accordion lanterns; paper heads of cattle; a plethora of painted flowers blowing in the breeze like the most generous dispersions of nature; geometric shapes hanging in the breeze, weaving a message that declared order and truth amidst change. With these paper words uttered by the Spirit, the Indians gave thanks for what was good in their lives, their livelihood, their capacity to love and to bless in a wholly natural way beyond thought. The three women felt simple, human and part of a whole that diminished no one. I see now why they think they've become Indians, Lynne thought.

The service was composed only of singing and a reverent silence of bowed heads and private prayers unattended by a priest, for the priests were ministering to wealthier congregations. The three women left with the Indians and returned to their homes to celebrate the evening with candles in the living room. They drank dark Mexican beer, Lynne's favorite, and waited for the children to arrive and receive the gifts they had bought them. After a few hours, Josefina and Blanca arrived with their three daughters, who were breathless with excitement over the new experience of receiving Christmas gifts from gringas. They sat in front of a small Bohemian glass Christmas tree that Red and Jean had bought in Prague and always placed on the living room mantle every Christmas. The gifts were large decorated boxes on the floor below the glass tree.

"Can we open them right away?" Clara asked.

"Of course," Jean said, and all the women smiled. Clara unwrapped a box of candy and a huge stuffed bear whose staid brown eyes seemed proud of his imposing, furry immensity. Teresa received an elaborately tooled European music box, a silk scarf and a box of candy. Nieves received a box of candy, a stuffed lamb whose black eyes glowed with tenderness, and a stuffed bunny with a wild, childish expression that seemed an invitation to leap along with it. They shouted their joy over the gifts and began hugging and marveling over them while eating their candy.

"I have only one gift, besides the candy," Clara said, "though it is a very big one. So, they got more than I did."

This was the kind of conundrum that Lynne enjoyed. "But what can be more or greater than a bear? In comparison to a huge bear, there can be no more desire for anything else, wouldn't you say?"

"I had not thought of that," Clara said. "A bear *is* a whole lot to receive."

"Besides," Jean added pragmatically, "there are more gifts in the next room." The three girls scrambled up and ran into the next room, then screamed and shrieked as though their souls were being stolen.

"Now *that* is Christmas praise!" Red said. The girls returned to the living room with shiny new bicycles. Nieves alone looked disturbed, nearly unhappy.

"What is it?" Blanca asked.

"Well, we have so much. We've never had a Christmas like this before. Why should we have so many gifts? Maybe from now on, we'll cry every Christmas because it will never be like this one."

This was the sort of conundrum Red enjoyed. "There are no other children here, so we have extra gifts. And, the gifts are from the Christ child, who knows the most wonderful gifts of all. You would never refuse gifts from the Christ child, after all."

"Yes," said Clara with determination. "The Christ child gets gifts at every fiesta, on so many fiestas each year. "I've had to give him so many of my toys and candy that I should get plenty back. That's how I see it."

"That's true!" Teresa said. "The Christ child is *fat*! I've never seen one that isn't really fat. The Virgin should put him on a diet."

"Yes!" Nieves said with astonishment. "I've never seen a statue of a Christ child that didn't have a big round belly, fat arms and legs and a double chin, and I'll even have to give him some of my candy tomorrow morning."

"I'm going to put him on a diet tomorrow," Clara said. "I'll keep all my candy. His mother won't do it because virgins are weird, especially the ones who have children."

"That's a good idea," Teresa said. "I'll keep my candy, too. But, what will we begin with among all these toys?"

This was the type of practical conundrum that Jean was always content to solve. "You'll sleep with your first gifts and ride the bicycles tomorrow," she said.

"Oh, that will be so wonderful!" said Nieves.

"And remember, the Christ child never got to do that. You're the lucky ones," Red said.

"I want to sleep with my bear now," Clara said. "He's so big that I can't even hold him in my arms. I will have to be held in his, which will be something that has never happened before." She placed her bear on the floor and lay in his furry armpit with her head on his shoulder, her arm over his chest. "This is a very nice, well-behaved bear."

The women talked for a short time, shared wine and beer, and soon the Mexican women and their daughters left. They expressed gratitude but were obviously very tired. "How are your businesses going?" Jean asked.

"I've sold Christmas decorations to almost everyone in the village," Blanca said in obvious fatigue.

"I've sold a dinner to just about everyone, too," said Josefina, closing her eyes in dismay at so much repetition.

Mothers are always exhausted by the holidays, Lynne thought, victims of Christmas all the world over. Red, Jean and Lynne had a wine nightcap in a last moment of appreciation. Beside her bedroom door, Lynne said, "This is probably my favorite Christmas, for which I thank you. I think I've had more new impressions than this holiday has ever given me in the states."

"We'll do another Mexican Christmas next year," Red said. "You'd love the Day of the Dead, too."

In the morning, the three women woke up late with a smile. As they came into the living room, they were greeted by a house full of women with tense faces. The three girls were there, too. "They won't let us go out and ride our bicycles," Clara said angrily. "We have to stay here. Isn't that mean?"

The three women instantly knew that another Mexican woman had been killed during the night.

And, now I know why they said they had lost the 'big picture', Lynne thought. The truth hits you like a van down here.

DIEGO WAITED WITH a pup tent in the forest on Christmas Eve. He was beside a large group of bushes and made sure his outline blended in. He looked at his drum, the one thing he had brought besides the tent. Uncontrollably, his mind replayed the tormenting scene of the previous night he had spent in the filthy bar. He had wanted a woman, and there was one seated in the bar. "Whatever you charge for a fuck, I've got it," he said as he approached her. The woman rose and walked to him. He quickly pushed her up against the wall and separated her legs as he had seen the other men do. He wanted to be one of those unknown, careless men, lunging at a woman, taking her roughly in the dark. Her face was strangely tranquil, which confused him. He handled her crotch and felt that she had no underpants on.

Then, a great, dark fury overcame him and he entered her vagina brutally, his face next to hers, dark, dirty and sweating. He put his hands on the wall beside her and made no effort to stimulate her. She held onto him, which again was unusual: she should have hated and feared him, he thought. He pushed her legs even more widely apart and shoved himself into her again and again. Now, he thought, now I'm as alive as I'll ever be, shoving it into a woman. This is how I live now. This is who I am. Just a prick that's found a hole, and it feels damned good. He moved further into her and thrust his pelvis again and again, which relieved his fear more than anything else he knew. A slew of foul words ran through his mind, and he thought, great, great.

Then a glass crashed to the floor near him and he went flaccid. Still inside the woman, he looked at her face in terror. Her face looked mildly into his own dark, sweating face, and they breathed together. Incredibly, she seemed to understand everything. "You're safe," she whispered. "No one ever looks in a dark corner where a man is fucking a woman." In his terror, shame and delirium, he began to cry softly. He wept on her breasts and kissed them tenderly again and again. He touched her as softly as he would touch silk and he did not get hard again. They stayed lying together in the corner all night. She caressed and calmed him as though nothing unusual was happening. He kissed her fingers and toes and made love to her orally, in spite of all the men she'd been with.

When first light rose in the sky, he said to her, "I will marry you, and you can leave this. Will you take me as your husband?" He was shocked by his words. Nothing he did or said now made any sense.

"What awful thing have you done?" she asked.

"I can't say."

"Then I can't marry you."

"Can you stand me? Am *I* awful?"

"It doesn't matter. You can hide here, with me." Slowly, he realized that the woman had felt empathy for him, from the beginning. She had sensed his fear, frustration and pain. She knew he was damned, and she freely offered her comfort.

When the dawn first streaked the sky, he kissed her fingers again and put the whole contents of his pocket into her hands, a lavish sum. She nodded her head at the sum as if confirming something and did not smile. "Amigo," she said, "You have done something truly terrible."

"I know," he said, stumbling to his feet and leaving her, walking unsurely out the door and into the terrible beginning of light. His mind was more and more confused, but he knew he must get home.

The memory now ended, and Diego was in the forest again, staring at his drum. He began to drum for Carlos and thought, it will be easy tonight. It's Christmas Eve. The goons will be drinking and warm somewhere with a woman. They won't be looking for me, or not as carefully. It will be the same for Christmas Day. Some might even be in church, god forbid. Tonight, he would have time to get home far before dawn. Still, he knew that he must be on his guard. They should all know by now that strange things happened in the forest.

In a half-hour, Carlos leaped out of the trees in his grey unitard and sat beside Diego. "You've been hiding yourself. It's been a long time. Why?" Diego said nothing and again Carlos asked, "Why?" He paused, then said, "I've recovered nearly all of my memory." Diego looked at him in terror. Carlos' face looked dark and vicious. "*You* look *awful*," Carlos said to Diego.

Diego cried out, "I'm afraid of the Dark God."

Carlos knew this to be untrue. "I know what's happening, you stinking *brujo*. You give me drugs, and I kill women for you." He punched Diego in the face.

"So you know, then. We really are damned. Why did you come back to me?"

"It's worth it," Carlos said with the most ominous face of all. It was almost unreadable in its intensity, like that of a god. His eyes glittered like a beast, like the most terrible insanity. He punched Diego in the face again, but no more.

Diego bled onto his shirt and asked, "What will you do now?"

"I'm not afraid of the Dark God. I want him above all else. It's worth a woman's life. If I have to choose between civilized behavior and the Dark God, I want the god. He can kill me tonight if he wants to. I've lived millions of years, Diego. I've built other universes and lived in them, seeing them begin and end. Can you possibly imagine what that's like, Diego? The beauty, the power of it!"

"You fool!" Diego said. "I've given you mezcal laced with the most powerful hallucinogen that exists and added meth so that it hits you all at once. None of what you've seen is real! Nothing! It's pure delusion, you fool!" It was the first honest conversation they'd even had, Diego reflected.

"Yet, you know you've opened a cosmic doorway. I was in your mind when you thought it. I've been everywhere, in every mind. You know it, and there's no turning back. You can't shut the door; only the gods can. Besides, stop shouting and looking so vile. My grandfather's hit men have been looking for you everywhere. You're a dead dog. It could be just hours away. Enjoy yourself, dead man."

"So, we're both damned. We both die like dogs." Diego had his mezcal in a bottle, and he opened it impulsively and drank liberally from it himself.

"Enough. Your stinking hide might just stay alive for a while somewhere, dark and crazy and miserable as hell. I'm giving everything up for it. This world is as damned and foul and stinking as you are. And, women have given me everything they can. I'll go happy, you bastard, and you'll die in agony."

So you're even sated, Diego thought. Again, the lucky boy, the favored one. You've had it all with many women, and I haven't satisfied myself a whit. You fuck while I masturbate or go flaccid inside a woman. "So, go to your death, you fool. Go down to damnation! I'll hand it to you." He gave the bottle to Carlos.

Carlos drank it all quickly. "Poor Diego," he said with the smile of a wolf. "He has to stay sane. He can't come and play with the gods." With that, he vaulted into the trees.

Who is sane and who not? Diego thought. He's just a monster. So am I. How does sanity apply to a monster? The forest had suddenly expanded, become a wilderness, endless, a continent. He was alone in a universe of trees and flowers, all shadow, like the early earth, when there were gods but no men. He knew he was hallucinating, and he decided to attempt the long walk to his house. He took his drum but forgot the tent.

He remembered the dark house where he had first met Carlos. It was now dark like that house and its forest. The dark of cosmic sight was never pure darkness. It was full of innumerable things, moving, crying, devouring, dying, all softly so that only the man devoured by darkness can hear and see. There were red-eyed demons here and they breathed their hot life into his face. Terrified, he gasped and then began to laugh. The demons did nothing, just glowered, and he lost his fear. He was safe, especially so, in hell. That's where he was, wasn't he? He had a terrific hard-on and clutched a bush, a tree, anything, and finally masturbated until it was gone. What an aphrodisiac these drugs are, he thought. What can be wrong with a place like this? But, he needed a woman. He always did, even in hell.

In the dark, so many living things, the whole dark wilderness, moved and the inconceivable light that was not light glittered from their bodies as they moved. Demons and animals were copulating, then the demons ate the animals in spidery patterns and splashes of shadow. He saw the masks of the most violent gods, and these were eaten by giant insects. Well, this was close to the world he knew: men lived to copulate and eat animals; then they, in turn, were eaten by smaller animals or by fire. Relative to this, the gods might as well be eaten by insects, for they offered only violence, neither comfort nor satiation. It had always been so, from the beginning of time. The world was so much like this dark world. He saw black churches, a black wooden bridge and a town square, black palaces with iron bars, and he recognized his own village. But now, it was as it truly existed—full of demons and animals. He was the only human being, and he winced in pride at that. It all repeated before his eyes: copulation, then eating, even cannibalism, over and over, until it all disappeared into shadows, death, nonbeing. Where was he? What was this? The world, he thought. Eternity, he thought. If hell, it was hell on earth, what men and animals must do, forever.

As he stumbled through the village, he looked into the windows of buildings. In one, he saw his father who had died, but here he was alive, naked and chained to the ceiling, grimacing in pain, terror on his face. This pleased Diego; his father had beaten him almost daily. He went in the door and found that it was a dark, filthy bar much like the one in which he had spent the last night. He looked around for blunt instruments but found only liquor bottles. That was enough. He broke them over his father's head and then used the glass' sharpness to gore this hanging flesh to a chaotic red pulp while his father screamed and begged for mercy. He left the body looking like a cow's dead body, hanging on a hook. It would be eaten by demons, he thought. He felt wonderful.

Perhaps this was the village of his dreams, the life of freedom he had dreamt of, the paradise. He walked through more of the black village. In another window, he saw his mother, naked and crawling on the floor. He had hardly known her, but in all his memories, she was brutal, a witch. She was gone one night, and he knew that his father had killed her. They never mentioned her again. "Help me, Diego," she said. "I can only crawl on the floor, and demons fuck and ride me all the time. Help me to my feet!" He only walked away.

He came to another bar of a pure blackness he could, incredibly, see through; it was transparent black, impossible. He entered and ordered whiskey that was oily in its blackness, again glittering from the light that was not light. He drank it down with relish, then looked into the corners of the room, those places he had huddled in for safety. He didn't need that now, oh no! He was safe in hell. He was on a par with everything, all utterly damned, the place no one made it out of. Seen from a distance, he imagined it as a great beast's maw, black and glittering within. There was a mirror behind the bar top, and he looked at his face. A red-eyed demon stared back at him. I'm wearing another mask, he thought, and touched it, intending to remove it, but it stuck to his face. It was his own flesh, he realized, his true face, which made him laugh uncontrollably, then he went into the corner. Was it worse to be a demon or to be killed by goons, he asked himself. Better to be a demon by far!

But something was missing. He needed a woman. How was it a holiday without what he always needed? The corner fogged over, and a naked woman with a demon face came out. I don't mind the face, he thought; I only want the hole. Again, he threw her roughly against the wall and shoved himself into her. A glass broke behind him, but he only laughed and stayed hard. Oh yes, he thought. This is how it should have been last night! Fucking a woman against a wall, hard all night. What better world could there be? None! This was the paradise. What Carlos did was foolish, unreal. This was the right cosmic doorway to cross. Carlos had crossed the wrong threshold; he, Diego, was with the world's true gods.

In the morning, he found himself wandering along the highway that led to his house. He was not far from it and realized that he must have been walking all night. He had his drum but had left the tent behind. His terror was muted by the residual effects of the drugs. When he stumbled into his house, he looked immediately into a mirror and saw the remnants of the demon face. A demon was powerful. Who would try to kill it? He found some comfort in this thought. He removed his clothes and relaxed in his bed. A disturbing question suddenly came to him: had he remembered to bury the woman's body? No, probably not. They would find the tent and the woman and think he was the murderer. Well, that could not increase the danger he faced. Nothing could do that. He remembered his dark, glittering night journey. The dark he had seen was the real world, and nothing is darker than black. Black was the sum of all colors and therefore the sum of the world. His last thought was that it was Christmas day, the worst of his life, and undoubtedly the last. He would be dead soon, as would Carlos, but they would take some more women with them.


ON CHRISTMAS DAY, Alvaro was being restrained by two of Javier's hit men, and they were very good at their work. He sat bound and gagged in a chair like a gangster, making incoherent, angry sounds that only wet his gag. He had again shouted that he was going to kill Carlos, and it looked as though he would do it. Javier sat talking in the next room with Dr. Molina, sorting out what they did and did not know. "What can I do?" Javier asked. "They've looked everywhere. There's not a street or sewer within fifty miles they haven't gone into." He emitted a short laugh. "I think they've picked up every damned rat and looked up its ass. What has he done, gone into the jungle?"

"No," Molina said. "He can't murder women from there. He's hiding in plain sight as a person we wouldn't recognize. This time, they've found both a tent and a woman's body. He's here and he's getting careless, which will work to our advantage. What do the *brujos* say?" As a boy, he had once seen a *brujo* perform a miraculous cure for which he had never found an explanation.

"Those fools say he's hiding in hell, covered with feces."

Molina looked up in consternation. "What do they say about Carlos?"

"That he's becoming a master of universes, but not this one. Does that make the slightest bit of sense to you?"

"No, none whatever. But, sometimes they make sense on another level, like monks in meditation. Be sure to pay them. Stop threatening. And, keep your henchmen looking for him. He has some sort of disguise. I should leave now and bring back some tranquilizer shots for Alvaro. We shouldn't leave him like that."

At that moment, the stocky Indian who led the operation was walking with another of Javier's hit men in the very town in which Diego lived. They were walking on every street and checking every cantina. Finally, they stopped in the filthiest bar of all, the one that seemed to be disintegrating back into the forest, the one in which Diego had spent the night before Christmas Eve. They entered the bar, and the Indian said in a loud voice, "We're looking for a man who has killed lots of women, women he doesn't even know. He's young, dark, big and heavy, and we have this very old photo of him. We'll pay anyone well for information on him. But, don't tell us any lies because we shoot liars."

In a bar like this, no one was surprised by statements or acts of violence. They passed the photo around calmly, but it bore little resemblance to Diego, the man who frequented their bar. A woman gave a start when she heard the man's crimes and considered letting them know about the strange man who had hired her for sex two nights ago and then cowered and cried in a corner with her instead. He had clearly done something terrible and feared that men were coming for him. Still, she remained silent. I've known too many men and *all* their dirty secrets, she thought; but I've never known a man who would cry and cower in a corner with a woman, then propose marriage to her, and yet murder an unknown women a few hours later. They're plenty perverse, but not like that, she thought. Still, she felt very uneasy about that strange man.

Back on the street, the Indian and his friend saw a particularly dirty, disgusting beggar sitting on a street corner. He appeared insane and passive, talking softly to himself and smelling of feces. If they had looked more carefully, they might have found Diego; but like everyone else, they quickly turned away from the smell of a man covered with feces. Everyone in town avoided the street corner. Diego wanted to see who was looking for him and in fact looked sharply at what was going on. If he saw Javier's hit men, he might be able to avoid them. From a distance, the operation leader considered the filthy beggar. "I bet that animal over there sees everything passing by, day or night. Go to him and show him the photo."

His partner was disconcerted by the task and the smell. "But he's loco. He only sees what's in his head."

"Never mind. We have nothing to lose. Show him the photo." The man frowned and walked toward Diego. He gave him the photo and asked the inevitable question. To his surprise, Diego smiled and nodded. The operation leader, in excitement, ran up to them. Diego lowered his head humbly, reached into his crotch and smeared feces on the photo with a smile. The two men shouted and jumped away, not bothering to retrieve the photo. In that second, Diego's crafty face looked up and memorized their features.

"Well, *damn* that idiot!"

"Loco, I told you. He doesn't know what you say to him or what he's doing. If he did, he'd smell better."

"Bloody hell! Now the photo's gone," said the operation leader. "You know, when it gets dark, I'm going to give this town a holy month gift. I'm going to put a bullet into that crazy bastard's skull."

At dusk, the operation leader and his partner came back in their car. The leader was so furious that he couldn't wait for nightfall to kill the beggar. He saw Diego's outline on the street, aimed and cocked his gun. "Wait a minute," the other man said. "I just thought of something: then we'll have to bury him. We'll have to actually pick him up and move him, probably in this car. That'll be even worse. We'll throw up. If we kill him and leave him there, he'll look and stink even worse by morning, his arms and legs partly eaten by starving dogs. Some holy month gift!"

The operation leader shouted a long string of expletives and shot three times into the air in rage as their car roared away from the impossible situation.

A FEW HOURS later, Diego returned to his house, entered by the rear door, took a long shower, and rubbed himself with men's cologne. Then he started his drinking for the night. It was so close, he thought, but now I know what they look like. The rest of his thoughts were incoherent. I'm starting to lose my sanity, he thought, but at least I'm alive. He wondered whether that empathetic woman was at his bar tonight, and he could spend the last hours of Christmas Day safely with her. Madonna of the Filth, he thought; that's what I'll call her. When he arrived at the bar, he was told that she had left for good and said to tell no one of her whereabouts. Diego nodded in a deliberately casual manner, drank two whiskeys laced with rum, and left. Well, that's our stinking holy month for you, he thought. Not even the Madonna bothers to show up.


IT WAS EARLY evening, and Lynne Lonidier was sitting in Red and Jean's living room with a mug of dark Mexican beer, taking a brief respite after a long day. I have seen what I could never have imagined, she thought. There are rooms here with six hammocks stretched across their ceilings and seven mattresses below. They could be sheltering most of the women in this village. There are women sitting and lying on the mattresses or floors in some rooms, lost in conversation with one another as though they were in a college dormitory or a slumber party. Red and Jean buy guns for those who want them. Wonder of wonders: an unknown guerilla war between the sexes is going on down here, led by my librarian friends, financed by the State of California pension fund for librarians. It is too paltry to call my friends heroines of the revolution. They are giantesses, achieving the impossible, dwarfing the great Mexican generals and mythic *bandidos*, Bolivar to Villa.

Our work is now strictly defined. My Spanish is only a bit better but even as the mute poet, my job is to keep an eye on the women and children and try to intuit their needs. Red is now supervising the builders, and Jean is agonizing for us all, trying to solve the problems presented by a dwelling of so many occupants. A woman named Pepita, dark and lovely in her traditional dress, is captivating us all. She has the brightest eyes I've ever seen and tells spellbinding stories that she says are part of Mexican culture. She lights a candle and sits before all the children, then raises her finger to the wind. Her finger moves to the rhythm of the candle's flame as though the stories come from it, a sign of the power of tales and their mysteries. She knows the rhythm so well that she doesn't even have to watch the candle. Then, before us is a Mayan girl named Rosha who has the longest shining black hair in the village. She once played with her older brother but is now old enough to want to play her own games and invent her own fantasies. He is enraged and cuts her long hair that very night, enmeshing the sun so it cannot rise and give the world light and fertility. Pepita's hands move in a circle and her fingers clench as the sun is entrapped.

The life of the world now depends on Rosha, she says, who tries and fails to release the sun. Then, she rushes to the forest animals for help. They refuse her, all but the least important —a tiny mole. When she returns, the mole's insignificance is a strength: it can leap the fastest on its small pink feet and not be burned by the sun, and it can cut all the hair's snarls with its tiny teeth. Pepita's hand draws the same circle with her fingers moving swiftly like the mole. The sun is saved, and in gratitude rewards Rosha by placing flashing sunlight in the eyes of all Mayan women, and it allows the mole to live safely forever beneath the ground. It is over in the movement of candle light, and Pepita's hands return to her lap. She does not have to say, resist the tyranny of men and boys. Look for unlikely allies; great things depend upon small ones. Watch and learn, for only women will save the world.

In another moment, Pepita's finger rises again, sign of the sacred, and a Hungry Goddess enters the room. She lives at the beginning of time, before the earth exists. There is nothing but water and the magic of gods. The gods are beautiful and full of power, but they have no desire to make the earth and its life. There is Quetzcoatl in his eagle-faced mask, his cape of many colors, and magic wand in the shape of a serpent, for he will always be known as the Plumed Serpent. Here is Texcatlipoca, also impressive with rattlesnakes around his legs and on his foot, a magic black mirror that can see all that exists, for he will always be known as the Dark God. But the Hungry Goddess cries for more; she is crying for the earth to be born. I'm hungry. I'm hungry! she cries. Pepita lays her head back and opens her mouth with her hands raised and open. Such is the hunger this goddess had for the earth and life to begin. The gods do not know what to do, try to calm her with their male strength, and break her in two by accident, creating fear and horror among all.

But here, now, is the earth. Half of the goddess becomes the sky and the other half, the earth. Her hair whirls into forests, tumbling with animal life. From her mouth spring great rivers and lakes, full of shining fish and frogs. Pepita gestures in like motion to each part of her body as the great transformation takes place. The goddess' skin becomes grasses and effusions of flowers; her nose, caves. From her hips grow huge mountains, and her stomach becomes the valleys before them. All living things and their world depend upon this goddess; yet still, she is hungry. The rain is the goddess drinking and all things that die and fall to the earth are her food. This she eats and creates new life. Pepita raises her finger as she speaks and traces the rhythm of life. Her message is unspoken: power may seem to be in the hands of men, but the reality of the earth resides in women. Men congratulate and glimmer, but women are revelation and regeneration.

Again, Pepita's hands return to her lap. The house is completely silent; all children and their mothers are listening, expectant.

Then, as the wind rises, so does Pepita's finger, as though she is obeying a command from the earth. In the room, now, are the Zapotec people of southern Mexico and Tehuantepec, who believe they have been visited by a great goddess named Tangu Yuh. She appeared to them on two New Years' Days, years apart, they say. She is a beautiful, towering giantess in a purple flowered dress and purple flowers and fruit in her hair, even as the Zapotec women dress today. Lightning and thunder accompany her descent to earth, and she is heralded by winged women flying in the air, blowing trumpets. Why did she come? The gods believed that the people lived harmoniously and should be rewarded by a goddess, for harmony flows from goddesses. But, the gods were wrong. All the Zapotec people worked and felt equal; that much was true. In the north, women wove cloth and embroidered textiles and men hunted deer, boar and iguanas to eat. In the south, both men and women were artists, making clay pots, drums and flutes, which they played to create music while they worked. In the center of the land, women ran the markets and handled the money while men carried the Zapotec goods over mountains and rivers to trade for necessities. All worked and were equal, but no one felt they could violate these laws of livelihood and create new things and ideas. So, when Tangu Yuh arrived in their city, they ran to her helter-skelter and tried to leap over one another to touch her, for she was both a goddess and a being newly created outside of their laws.

Then, the goddess knew that they did not live in harmony; she left them, but she was a goddess and felt what they felt. She did not want them to suffer and live without hope. So, she came again, also on New Year's Day. Now, today, there is always a fiesta among the Zapotecs on New Year's Day. They make dolls that look like Tangu Yuh and celebrate with food and music. They have never given up hope that she will come again. Here is the only time Pepita intervenes with reality. The same is true today, she says, the Zapotec women are very powerful and control all the markets and commerce of their people. They are great leaders in this.

Pepita's hands return to her lap and she looks down. It seems as though the performance is over, but she listens, waiting, and the wind rises again and the candle's flame dances. She looks up and asks a question: how is it that the sun and moon are always so far apart and rule over domains as different as day and night? Many people have wondered about this, she says, and there is an old story about why the moon has her freedom. Once, you see, the sun fell in love with the moon and wanted to marry her. Like all men, he was hot, desirous and wanted to control what he loved. The moon was so pale and beautiful that he thought he could not live without her. But the moon was a woman with a mind and life of her own for look, here, she talked all the time to stars and the life on planets made her laugh all night. Think of how you would love that life of the moon—forever talking and laughing, feeling everything, forever beautiful and in communion with all that is. Think how she would laugh at what goes on here on earth. I bet you can imagine that! she says and the children laugh. Pepita's hands become the moon, round and looking about and the sun, hot and enflamed.

The moon didn't want to marry the sun, since he was so hot and busy and needed her so much. But, he was very powerful and she had to outwit him. So, she said she would marry him only if he could dress her in the most beautiful clothes. The sun thought, how like a woman, vain and caring only how she looks. He did not know he was being tricked, so he took her measurements and made one dress after another, only to find that it no longer fit her. She had expanded or shrunk. So, the moon is still free, even today, and she laughs at both the sun and life on earth and talks all night to the stars. Not another word from Pepita is necessary. The tale has said it all: freedom is lovely, not frightening, and the same is true of self-sufficiency.

Then, Pepita asks the children, what did that beautiful lady, the moon, look like? The youngest child makes a great circle with his arms and falls backward, laughing. The youngest laugh with him. The older children draw circles everywhere, seeing gravity and orbiting moons around their planets and stars. Nieves draws a circle that becomes two hands on which she appears to sleep. Only Clara, annoyed, says that the moon looked like an airplane pilot in her general's uniform, to which everyone laughed. The children are now ready for bed, and their mothers smile knowingly at one another. Pepita has been thoroughly subversive, a liberator. When she raises her finger again, there will always be silence in this house.

On the next night, the children ask to hear more about those big, strange girls and women who do wonderful things, and Pepita said, I do know a few more stories. She lights the candle and sits with her hands in her lap again, listening to the moment when the wind rises and the candle's flame dances. Then she raises her finger and allows it to move with the flame's rhythm. I know a story about a woman who became a green bird, she says. It is from the Zapotec people who live in Oaxaca. In the old times when magic was practiced all the time, there was a Zapotec king named Great Jaguar. This king was very powerful and had control over much land, but it was never enough. He wanted his beautiful daughter, Kesne, to marry a rival king's son, so he could control that king's wealth and land also. His wife, Serpent Goddess, did not approve of this, nor did his daughter, for she was already in love with another man named Tidacuy. When Kesne refused to marry the rival king's son, the enraged king used sorcery to turn her into a green bird. Though beautiful, this green bird was frightened and ashamed of her new body and hid in the forest. The forest animals protected her, for they hated injustice and suffering as much as we do.

Well, the king didn't live very long. Those who want power so much that they cause suffering rarely live to old age. Kesne's mother, Serpent Goddess, used sorcery again to restore Kesne to her human body, but she needed the help of the forest birds. All acts by people depend upon the earth and its creatures, which is why we must live without hurting them. So, the forest birds allowed Kesne to return to her people and become their queen. She married Tidacuy, and a time of rejoicing followed. Serpent Goddess and Kesne were happiest of all then, and they had a wonderful new power besides magic. They could hear the thoughts of the most beautiful birds—the hummingbirds, the turtle doves, and the toucans. The magic of animals, you see, is very great. Kesne and her mother were happy because they knew what the forest knew: don't fear change and transformation; wisdom comes from hidden places; life and the world are stranger and more amazing than you think.

Pepita's hands return to her lap. The children look at one another in wonder and then laugh at the strangeness of what they've heard. Is there another big girl who can do anything, they ask. Pepita is silent, seeming to consider the question deeply. Oh, that would be the devil's daughter, Blanca Flor. The children make an ahhh of surprise and nearly begin to talk to each other. Oh yes, Pepita says, this girl did exist, and the children are silent again. Blanca Flor's mother was the female devil and her father, the male devil. So, Blanca Flor was perfectly good since she had such parents, and she was a great shaman as well.

One child suddenly says, the devil lives in hell with flames and is bad. The priest says that.

But, the old stories and the old religions say otherwise, Pepita says, and they are more powerful. She does not have to say another word about their power; the room is silent, listening. Blanca Flor and her parents live in the air, Pepita says, and in the story, Blanca Flor falls in love with a man named Pedro, a gambler who had made a pact with the devil for more money to gamble away. As we know, gambling never pays. Our actions are always intertwined with the earth, and the earth can't ever be bought with money. Blanca Flor knew this and her magic saved Pedro. Then she married him and lived just like an Indian woman in a village with her husband. Pedro was a good man then who never gambled. So you see, devils aren't any more evil than you and me, just different. Contact with the supernatural, even devils, can purify. I bet you didn't know that.

But the priest doesn't say that, the child said again.

Of course not, said Pepita. The old religions know the same thing that the forest knows in the story of the green bird that became a queen. They know that the world is a stranger and more wonderful place than you think. You will always be changing and learning new things and actually, you like living in a world like this rather than reciting catechisms.

That's true, said Nieves. We like it better that way.

A quiet of wonder descends on the room. They don't have to ask for another story. When Pepita raises her finger, the quiet is a force, touching all. But, she prolongs the silence, and the children hear the sounds of the night more distinctly—the soft crying bark of a distant coyote, a faint, curious kree-kik-kik of a falcon, a wind that does not flow but seems to flutter through the dense, pendant foliage of the Mexican oak. Pepita's finger grows in power. Without speaking, she conveys that stories make you more aware of the world around you: its ceaseless motion, it unknowability, its mystery.

Suddenly, she begins again, as though the night sounds have given her a special strength. The Aztecs told the story of a brilliant princess named Malintzan who spoke all the languages known then—Nahuatl, Mixtec, Mayan. When the Spanish conquerors came, she learned Spanish from Cortez. But, when she saw his cruelty to her people, she cried so much that she disappeared in the river of her own tears. This river took her to a great mountain, Texocatepic. The people who lived on the mountain were called Hahuaques, and they could summon the power of rain and thunder to make crops grow and the earth become fertile. That is a great power, and the mountain life was very wild, full of so much rain, thunder and lightning. Malintzin lived with the mountain people in caves. When the Spanish soldiers tried to conquer her people, Malintzin had learned the powers of the mountain and sent thunder and lightning to kill the generals of the militia.

She is now a huge woman, very beautiful, with many jeweled necklaces that flash with the power of thunder and lightning. Many Indians think she has become the mountain, for she and the cave people give strength and courage to Malintzin's people by beating drums that sound like thunder. But, Malintzin is even greater than the mountain because of her empathy. When her people suffer, she cries streams of tears to make the earth fertile. That's why the most beautiful flowers are at the base of the mountain; they have been watered by her first tears. Even now, she is a great and powerful woman who lives forever, like a goddess. Pepita's finger rises and her power seems to fill the room. She does not have to say that women have always resisted male tyranny and so must you. The spell has been cast, and the children merely wait. Teresa finally asks, who is the greatest woman of all?

That's hard to decide, says Pepita, since there have been so many great women. But, I think you already know her story, the Virgin of Guadelupe, the dark-skinned goddess who appeared before the boy, Juan Diego. As you know, she is the virgin mother of the people, and she protects them and is more powerful than the priests. But, you may not know the five questions she asked the boy, Juan Diego, the answers to which he knew immediately. They are good and wonderful questions, and they show the power of this goddess. She asked, am I not your mother? Are you not under my shadow and protection? Am I not your foundation of life? Are you not in the folds of my arms? Is there anything else you need? Those are the kinds of questions a powerful woman would ask and value most highly—the fact that we can answer them in our hearts. That is why this goddess has always been so much greater and more dear to us than the church.

Pepita then merely gets up and walks away, a bit like her goddess of intuition, Lynne thought. I have listened to her gifts for two nights, and she can make me wish that my poetry had her power. Several of the women have heard these stories, but they are entirely new to the children. Pepita is the only one who can keep Clara's rapt attention for any period of time; she has charmed our small cobra. The girls seem to be having the time of their lives. The world is quite a commotion, and their nights, filled to overflowing with imagination. I wish I could see into the minds of the women in this house. I thought I knew the story of Mexico, but they might teach me a new one.

I tell our stories full of magic and strong women, Pepita was thinking, and with that I help these women and children to beat back the dark. Yet, after sunset, it is always there: the shadows, the wind, the small soft cries of creatures somewhere between living and dying, the secrets, the terrors. In darkness, the world is full of were-jaguars. By day, we dream of good and the gods and honor them by dancing in our fiestas. But the dark is never defeated. Death is still beside us, ready to take another woman. The dark is an ancient, terrible quiet in which even monsters whisper as softly as the wind.

Maria, sitting on the floor meditatively, was thinking, just who are you, Mexico? Will every woman need to run her own business before this ends? I think we should be shouting our defiance everywhere, publicizing it, talking to the media. But, we have decided to act only in concert and my view is badly outnumbered. How can the murder of women be kept secret? It should be a scream heard all over Mexico!

I will protect these children with my mind, heart, soul and still more if it must be, Josefina was thinking. I will earn the money to take them out of here, and they will be the women they want to be. If I ever find these murderers, I will shoot them; but if I could, I would destroy them with my hands. My rage would turn me into another being, and as the true were-jaguar that can only be female, I would claw them into bloody pieces. So, Mexico, I do still touch your violent past in my deepest self as a mother. Josefina reached down to touch the gun she carried beneath her blouse. But you, amigo, I will go to first. How I would love to fire that first clean shot that demolishes all this chaos, fear and anguish caused by men.

The world is disintegrating all around us, Rosa was thinking, and what do I raise against it? Woven textiles, my only unity, the sole way my life comes together again. It may be a small thing, but it makes sense. My fingers move so fast that I hypnotize myself. It is how I have always coped with my husband. He's a drunk, and I suppose he will die soon, like the others. When he does, I will create his *ofrenda*: a textile cut in many pieces and an empty liquor bottle will lie upon his altar. Does he even deserve remembrance? Hardly. Nieves is so sensitive that I can't predict what she will become. The other girls have made her stronger, and she might reach for greatness like them or simply be a mother. Either is good enough for me. I am at peace if they are alive and well.

What is this world, Blanca was thinking, terrible and wonderful, but I am a sleeping dancer filling it with lovely images. My art is complete simplicity and spontaneity. Perhaps it is not so for a great artist, but I make crafts for sale as quickly as I can and even talk to friends while doing it. I am grateful that it flows so easily from me; it is a great gift. My art keeps me at peace and strangely enough, it seems to place me at the pace of the universe. It is a fanciful thought, for what do I know of the universe? Yet, it feels so. I fly and float upon my art, never soar. It is only that much, but that is enough.

At the end of the evening, quite late, the three Americans gathered in the living room for wine and talk. "Shouldn't we be trying to find out who it is?" Lynne asked. "There's the forest and the spring to decipher. The murders begin and end there. Are you up for some amateur sleuthing?"

Red and Jean only looked exhausted.

"Our hands are full here," said Red, "and you are not a person whom I would normally ask to 'get real.'"

"This is serious and draining," Jean said.

"But how can we know when it will happen again? Don't you want to know that?"

"Questions, questions!" Jean said. "We can't solve anything, only give all we can to these women and children."

"But, we don't seem to be living in a modern world here," Lynne persisted. "Shouldn't we adapt?"

"We *are* living in the modern world," Red said fiercely. "The abuse of women and children is the world's dirty secret, anywhere, Europe, America, anywhere. Period!"

They were silent for a long time, listening to the sounds of the night: wind, trees, animals, shadowy movement everywhere. "There are monsters in that wind," Lynne said. Questions, questions, Jean thought. Monsters! Red thought. What can anyone do but what we're doing?

JAVIER, ALVARO AND Dr. Molina were also sitting in their living room, discussing their quandary. "Carlos has aged again," Molina said.

"There's a nasty, wild look in his eyes," Alvaro said. "I think he likes the whole thing, killing, being drugged out of his mind, but he'll never say it, of course."

"Why haven't you been able to get more information out of him, like where he meets Diego, how he gets out of the house and so forth?" Molina asked.

"He says he remembers nothing. He always says that," Javier said.

"There is memory loss from the drugs, of course, but he should be having flashbacks," Molina said. "He should know quite a lot. They have some strategy, some way of getting together. It even preceded the drugs."

"That's what I mean about his liking it," Alvaro said. "He lies to us so it can go on. It's time to change *our* strategy. It's time for justice, vengeance. He can't be allowed his freedom. It's either jail or a mental hospital he can't get out of. I don't think it matters now. I can't imagine his ever becoming sane or harmless. He might as well be drugged into idiocy."

There was a long silence. "I'll start looking for a hospital," Molina said. "You might catch Diego by then, so something more positive could still happen."

"What should we do in the meantime?" Javier asked.

Where do you put a monster? Molina wondered. Perhaps where you put a woman who becomes insane or useless: the attic. "Fix up the attic. Fill it with his books and music. Put an outside lock on the door, and let him out only with two of your men. He's phenomenally strong. Put the rest of your men in the forest. Give up the search. Wait for Diego to come here." Molina thought of himself as the bridge between worlds, the arbiter. He was a medical man and had the power of clarity conferred by science, but he was also a man who had studied philosophy and literature, like Carlos. This may be the strangest case of my life, he thought. Questions, questions. Am I trying to treat the illness of a man, a country or the world?

The wind rose, and the three men looked around themselves suddenly as though they were haunted by a ghost or one of the old gods was peering at them from a dark corner.


NOW I'M A prisoner, Carlos thought, lying in bed, his hands behind his head. I must always act the part; they can't know how easily I can escape from the attic. Only in the dead of night, when I can't hear a single sound, can I go and lie on the roof and look at the universe, my real home, and remember the gods, my real family. They've put all my books and music here. That's barely decent of them. It's definitely the time to read all of Shakespeare, all of *The Remembrance of Things Past*, all of Scheherezade's tales. I'll read all the Latin American novelists who practice magical realism and all those American popular science books on string theory and alternate universes. It's my personal reality, after all. I'll spend long hours in gymnastics to work off all the frustration.

One of our hit men came in one night and said, "I'm looking forward to your escape attempt. I'll shoot you dead. I'm not so particular about rich boys. You just try it, golden boy. I haven't killed a man in some time, and my prick and trigger finger are getting itchy." Carlos smiled. The bastard almost drooled, he thought. Where do they find these monsters? Maybe the same place they got me. Does the world really make more sane men than monsters, and does daylight or dark change one into the other?

Javier and Alvaro are different toward me. They talk less about rehabilitation. They've probably lost faith, in which case they'll have Molina get me locked up somewhere. I will have to intuit the exact time so I can escape. O, darkness and freedom! What can you teach me of mere men? They have a god under their roof. I can probably escape no matter what they try to do. The Dark God rules this universe, not their silly politics and goons and bullets.


HE WAS RIGHT, Diego was thinking late on the same evening. My hide is saved and here it lies in another corner of abject misery, terror and humiliation. I've got a little more time. Thanks for nothing. Diego had overheard the story of the *gringas* who were offering shelter to all the village women who wanted it; this enraged him and he enjoyed thinking of how he would kill them, how to make it slow, terrifying and humiliating. Time seemed to have expanded. He had no idea what to do with himself. He had decided on the last holiday of holy month, Three Kings, as the time of the next murder. The *gringas* will come later. Maybe he would split the drugs with Carlos to make them both violent, he thought.

He could hardly wait until it was over. One day, as he was walking around his present town, he found a branch of the public library. This struck him as the perfect place to kill time. His mornings and afternoons could be loafed away here, his evenings in the dirty bar, both perfect hideaways. Who would suspect a murderer in a library; and as for that bar, anyone could be a murderer there, so he had opposite suits of camouflage. He began to enjoy both the library and the bar more. He was truly interested in all he read and felt the luxury of reading with no time constraints. The librarians would approve of him, a well-dressed man who wanted to improve his mind. Maybe he could fuck a librarian, too. The luxury of retrospect was his, too. I should have been a librarian, he thought. I'd fuck all those women in their glasses. Maybe this would never have happened. He made a mental note to add a pair of glasses to his disguise.

IT WAS JUST past noon of the last day of holy month, Three Kings, and Lynne, Red and Jean were walking through the forest. The house was not so full; a few women had returned home, and Lynne planned on returning to San Francisco after the fiesta. "I am still far from feeling safe," Jean said. "It happens on the fiesta days, and this is the last. A woman could die tonight, someone we haven't been able to reach."

"And it always happens here, in the forest," Lynne said. They had just arrived at the hot spring. "It's a lovely spot, really, and the hot spring with the marble frame is truly beautiful. I can't imagine who put the marble there."

"That's one of the most curious things of all. It's someone with money, and it suggests a rite that we know involves murder," Red said. They sat on the marble and looked long into the green depths of the spring, where shapes gleamed and vanished in the turbulent water like life and death.

"It's safe by day," Jean said, "and I have my gun."

"I do, too," Red said.

"Well good, because I don't," Lynne said. They smiled but were preoccupied by the strangeness of the place. "The forest is thick, dark and powerful," Lynne continued. "There is something weirdly natural about the fact that it empties into that old cemetery. I have the same feeling about this spring."

"You're playing amateur sleuth again," Red said sharply.

"No, just aimlessly responding, being what I am, a poet, scouting for patterns. This place seems natural because it's primitive and mythic, I think. That's why we respond as we do. The spring must be the passage to the world of the gods in their mythology, and they reach it in death. Everything is related here."

"I've thought that, too," Red said.

"It coheres, but murder is an unnatural part of it," Lynne continued, as though searching for words and concepts.

"Sacrifice," Jean said.

"It could give the murderer, particularly a crazy one, a false sense of protection. Given the mythic setting, with such deep roots into their folklore, an insane killer would think of himself as a god. That's what strikes me. He kills with a knife, and he is totally vulnerable to a gun. That means he'll eventually be killed by one of the women you've armed. It will stop, and you'll all be safe again."

They were silent a long time, feeling a strange combination of fascination and completion. "It's so damned beautiful," Jean said.

"How can I leave you after the holiday?" Lynne said. "You're fighting a war. You're facing a great mystery and god-forbid, a beautiful one."

"Beauty is amoral," Red said.

"Except in the hands of an artist," Jean said.

"Does the murderer find it beautiful, too?" Lynne asked.

"He's twisted, of course," Jean said. "We probably saw him once, standing with a hard-on in a tree. He probably finds murder both erotic and beautiful."

"We revolve around and around the same mystery, and it even calms us, like the presence of great beauty," Lynne said.

"That halt in breath, that drop in pulse," Jean said. "You know that you've touched absolute reality, the universe."

"You're both missing something," Red said. "You're no doubt too preoccupied with your visions of beauty. The forest has changed since we were here last. There's more garbage around and some spots reek of urine. I've seen movement here at night, lots of people, probably men. Someone has dispatched the troops. And, what the hell does that mean? Has someone paid off the police, or is it a private army of the wealthy? We're no longer the only ones looking for the murderer."

"You're absolutely right!" Jean said. "It's very different here in the forest! A lot of underbrush has been trampled. There's an empty cigarette box over there; and yes, I smelled urine somewhere, too. What does it mean?"

"Trouble in paradise and maybe some help," Lynne said.

They stayed awake all night, eventually sitting on the living room carpet, drinking coffee. "It's like the Day of the Dead," Jean said. "The living and the dead are intermingling. I'm so glad you're here, Lynne."

"But, we're waiting for a murder."

Red came in from a moment outside, her coffee cup still in her hand. "There's more motion in the forest, troops on the move! What do you think of that?"

"The game has definitely changed," Lynne said, "but we're no closer to the truth or to preventing a murder."

"But someone is," Jean said. "Someone knows a lot more about this than we do." In different words, they all thought: this could be the darkest night of our lives. How necessary that we're here together; we can face it that way. They stayed awake all night, drinking coffee and talking.

In the early morning, several women returned to the house with their blankets and abject looks on their faces. The three Americans looked at one another. The tale was told: another woman was dead, in spite of the army in the forest, in spite of their vigil, in spite of everything they held to be good and true.

IN THE EVENING of the Three Kings holiday, Carlos sat in the middle of his living room, his arms stretched out on a huge sofa and a pugnacious look on his face. Javier's palace was celebrating the fiesta with a posh PRI fund-raiser, and Carlos was drinking wine and feeling bemused and a bit bored. The god Adonis deigns to be present, he thought. Elena had been trying to sneak into the palace for days but was banned by Javier without explanation, which only further amused Carlos. His grandfather's goons and hit men were all over the room, seeming to celebrate and mingle but always with careful eyes on Carlos. We have a fund-raiser with a murderer as favorite son, Carlos thought with a smile.

The hit man who had expressed a desire to kill him sat with his jaw hardened and a twinkle of hostility in his eyes. Maybe I can get golden boy on the lawn away from the others, the man thought. He had put a silencer on his revolver in anticipation, and he planned on taking off for the jungle after the body was discovered. Carlos only grinned at him. It has always been a palace where murders are plotted, he thought; why not have them carried out, too? All palaces have been places where violent deaths were planned; such was the history of the inferior race. But, a god can't be overpowered by such trash as this drooling dog, he thought. I must be killed only by the Dark God, himself, as befits a human raised to godhead.

His eyes scanned the room and were suddenly filled with awe. A stranger to the PRI had just sauntered into the room with a smile, a tall stocky man with glasses in an elegant suit and tie and hair carefully brushed back. Carlos resisted the impulse to laugh out loud, for it would have been fatal. It was Diego carrying a bottle of what appeared to be champagne. Diego casually sat on the sofa at an angle to Carlos, close enough for them to talk without acknowledging one another directly, like strangers meeting for the first time and making polite small talk.

"I'm proud of you, amigo! This is the most outrageous thing you've ever done," Carlos said.

"The forest is now a war zone, full of your grandfather's goons pissing everywhere, so this is the only way in." The goons in the room looked carefully at Diego and decided he must be a wealthy PRI regular or one of Carlos' college acquaintances.

"Does that bottle contain what I think it does?"

"Oh yes, amigo."

"More outrage! I will be relieved when we're elsewhere, so I can laugh as long as I please." Carlos rose and got two silver steins so that the color and texture of the liquid could not be seen by others. They toasted one another's longevity with rapacious grins and drank.

"That's all until later," Diego said.

"Of course," Carlos said coolly, suppressing his laugh. "This continues to be the most outrageous thing you've ever done. Hiding in plain sight and drinking mezcal here is a stroke of genius. You are becoming more god-like. How have you acquired such originality and strength of character?"

"The same place you got it. Partly the brew and the rest you know well enough. We don't care whether we live or die, whether we're damned or not."

"Where do we meet for the rest of this lovely brew?"

"Outside, still on your lawn, the south quadrant where it meets the forest. I can still hide there. Be there in an hour."

Carlos laughed in spite of his effort to appear nonchalant and slightly bored. "There's a goon here who desperately wants to kill me, even talks about it. He'd love to be there and administer the final act, but I know how to evade him."

"Of course." I completely understand this goon's desire, Diego thought. I'd love to do it myself.

"Do you know how to get out of here?"

"Oh yes. I've broken in and out of here many times when I was a boy. I lived here more than in my father's hole. I'm as invisible and dexterous as you."

"I will have to go with you this time," Carlos said. "I think they're planning on institutionalizing me. When the night is over, I must go with you in your car to whatever wretched hole you've been hiding in."

"Good enough. I'll drive away and then park beyond the forest. It may take me an extra hour to walk back. So, the fun begins in two hours."

Carlos rose slowly and casually and began to interact with the guests. Diego finished his drink and slowly walked into another room of the party with a pleasant, expectant air, clearly at home in the atmosphere he had known since boyhood. The murderous hit man watched Carlos avidly and had completely missed Diego. Just leave, pretty boy, the man thought. You're right in my sights.

After an hour, Carlos claimed to have a headache and went up to the attic. His last carefully watched movement was to look over his shoulder and see the goon's disappointed face at the foot of the staircase, watching him enter the attic. Inside, he lay on top of his bed in convulsions of laughter until he heard the door being locked from the outside. Then he put on his grey unitard and carried several others on his arm. Live and die with elegance, he thought. Then he opened the window slowly and crept across the roof where none of his grandfather's army expected to see anything. He saw the dark movement in the forest, cigarettes being lit and then going out. He leaped to the first tree, hiding behind a large bough. From there, it was all ease and pleasure. No one ever expected a predator from the forest canopy.

At first light, Carlos and Diego met beside Diego's car. Both were as filthy and bloodied as the most primitive savages. Diego had tried to bury the body, then became fearful of being seen and given up, leaving it at the forest's edge. "Well, we look just like what we are," he said. Carlos smiled and got into the car. They drove in near-silence to Diego's house in the nearby town and entered by the rear entrance in the palest light. Carlos looked around his new residence. "Can you stand this place?" Diego asked.

"Oh yes," Carlos said, resting his bloody limbs on the edge of a chair. "We might just kill each other for entertainment in a place this small."

"So we might." Carlos was the first to shower, but both grinned with a loose grimace like jackals.

IN ANOTHER WEEK, Lynne was at the airport, saying goodbye to Jean and Red. "For the umpteenth time, I hate to leave you here, in the middle of a war."

"It's a war that will end," Red said. "A woman will shoot the killers and then it's all over."

"It's a secret war on top of it, outside of all their institutions and culture, beyond anything we think we know, a violent journey into the unknown."

"Too poetic. We're just fighting like Indians," Jean said. "They don't announce their intentions, either, just fight from the forest. It all happens in silence, and it always has. Women haven't been a part of it before." They embraced one another tightly.

"I don't know what to say, and that's maddening for a poet. You're the most courageous women I've ever known, and I didn't realize it before coming here. Your story begs to be told."

"So be Ishmael," Red said.

"I categorically refuse to be anyone's Ishmael. You've got to make it through this and tell me the story yourselves."

"We will. We've become warriors," Jean said.

"Amen to that," Lynne said. Now it was the moment to part. "I'll call every day . . . no, every night."

"We'll expect you and delight in it," Jean said.

"It will all be over by next Christmas, and you'll be our guest again," Red said.

"I still don't know what to say, godspeed and godwhatever."

"You're disgracing yourself as a poet with those words," Red said.

"This is quite enough to change my poetry forever." They embraced a last time, squeezed hands, and they hoped and doubted in equal measure that they would ever see one another again. Lynne boarded the plane with one look back. Be the fiercest of Indians, my exquisite friends, she thought.


ON THAT DAY, the forest was nearly empty but no longer pristine. The army had left garbage there for many days, and the sacred spring had become a urinal. Only animal eyes saw it. Diego and Carlos would never return.


ON THAT DAY, Javier, Alvaro and Dr. Molina were sitting alone together for the last time. "No one can find them," Javier said. "They've vanished."

"Good," said Alvaro. "Their drugs have run out, and they've finally gone into the jungle where they belong. They should live with other predators."

"They'll go mad together, fuck Indian women, probably die together," Molina said.

"We've lost Carlos, my only grandchild!" Javier said.

"It's not as though you weren't perfectly willing to allow more women to get killed to get him back," Alvaro said with words of such bitterness he pursed his lips in disgust. Javier was shocked. "Besides, we never had him, anyway. He was always mad, always a monster. Diego is, too. They belong together. They'll probably kill each other."

"Carlos had so much promise, so many gifts," Javier said, still grieving. "But he was so twisted, too, so perverse. He was damned. You're the philosopher, Molina. Isn't it true?"

"I'd be a fool to think otherwise," Molina said. Thank-god it's over, he thought, while I still have any values left. He looked at Javier and Alvaro in great sympathy. Their faces were so tragic as to be nearly paralyzed, effaced by strong emotions, blank. They don't have anything left but their money, Molina thought. They've been so close to damnation as to virtually lose their humanity. Can it ever return?

On that day, Carlos and Diego were sitting in the town library. It had been Diego's haunt, but now it was necessary; they were men too frustrated and violent to look each other in the eyes. But here was the solution, the wonderful pages of books, the life of the mind. Cervantes or blood, Diego thought. He searched for something to say, some bridge over the death sitting beside them. "We could have been librarians, you know. We wouldn't have ended like this." Carlos broke into convulsive laughter that eventually caught many eyes. Diego, in fear, asked him to leave with him immediately. "I told you not to draw any attention to yourself," he whispered outside. "That's a great hideout."

"So, don't say such farcical things," Carlos said, still laughing.

That night, they drank in the filthy bar. "Here, you can do anything," Diego said morosely. "Pick as many fights as you want. Fuck or kill someone." When they returned home at first light, still the jittery wolf's hour to Diego, they got into a fist fight and barely missed breaking bones. It was not the first time.

As they dropped, bloody, into bed, Diego said, "You started it. You bleach the sheets and pillow cases." The saner one had to make order. Carlos only continued to laugh. Not even the dark is safe anymore, Diego thought. There's that hyena in it.

I CONTINUED TO call nearly every day, Lynne Lonider wrote. I am now Ishmael, the final teller of the story. It is against my will; but fortunately, I am not, like Ishmael, the sole survivor. So, I can tell you that in another month, the house was finished and the last payment was made to the building company. Jean and Red now stood outside the miraculous, near-impossible thing, saw it whole and beautiful as a newborn child, a poem crafted painfully, with great care. The walls of windows now reflected the gentle Mexican sun, the lake, and a distant ring of small, riotously colorful houses like that fresh, eternal garland of flowers on an ancient, hoary head. Call it Eden. Death was still close; but after all, there was always a serpent in Eden.

They were alone in the house now. The women and children had returned to their homes, so they decided to hold a celebratory feast for the workmen and their families. On that day, in early twilight, they saw the small men now enjoying themselves with their wives and children, for there was abundant food for every hungry mouth. The wide-brimmed hats tipped to them; the long, embroidered skirts whirled effortlessly in a ring of dancers. With intense satisfaction, they noted new color on the mens' cheeks, more flesh and muscle on their bodies, no doubt the result of the generous lunches they had served each day. As the festivity progressed, they passed throughout the group and gave a special bonus payment to each man who had worked on the house. This seemed to amaze the men, as though they had never received a reward for work well done. As the twilight deepened to nightfall and the moon's reflection swayed over the lake like another dancer in the widening ring, for the magical light now pooled and doubled in the wall of windows, Jean remembered that night and festival so long ago when their dream began. Tears came to her eyes at the thought of this symmetry: was it the only way, she wondered, that any goodness ever came to this old, beleaguered world, in symmetry with degradation? Now it had not merely happened, a gift from other hands. They had created it.

Yes, that was worth something, I agreed, perhaps everything, as long as it lasts. Until the old world's top spins yet again, as so perversely it grins and spins, until the dice fall down. I did not say this to Jean, though we spoke by telephone a few days later. How do we say what's painfully inevitable but with a story, and those we live are coarse, rough things; mumbling and dirty, they putrefy in the heart until just the right heat, depth, pressure and age are reached, the deathly recipe, and then come roaring out, the cauldron of monsters: poetry. Oh yes, poetry roars, is monstrous, deafens with its truth, still filthy in afterbirth. Of such things, terrible and true, are dreams made.

And so, what followed was perhaps inevitable. A week later, in early afternoon as Jean was looking out the windows, she saw three of the workmen circling the house. Immediately, she went out and greeted them. To her dismay, however, she saw that they were again thin, dirty and disheveled. In but a few moments, it was clear that they were drunk as well. With fear and pity filling her stomach, she asked if they had found more work, to which they replied no, there was never any work in the town. The building was across the bridge, they said, and different crews were used for that area. Jean instantly felt anguish: the town's poverty and inequity had reasserted themselves. The men never had a chance. "I am so very sorry," she said helplessly in Spanish. Her anguish was unshared, however; they were now too drunk. A thought began, touched her with light fingers: what would it be like to fail, and then again, fall, fiercely hunger, stagger here, still wretchedly alive, like these men? Their eyes had a dark, strange fluidity—fatigue, anger, fever, utter blankness were there—all shifting, turning into one another. Eyes of the lost. She had seen such eyes before—in the craggy face of the Indian painter from Taos whose work was on several of their walls.

She took a deep breath of air; suddenly aware she had stopped breathing. The scene before her had now altered dangerously. The men stared at her boldly and laughed suddenly in derision, then they began talking among themselves, ignoring her entirely, all the while their eyes shifting, burning with fluid, fluent thoughts, too fast, too dangerous, for words. They used a slang term, apparently a reference to her, something that sounded like *moneymama*. Stunned and embarrassed, she went inside and locked the door. What now? That was the awful question still turning, fluid, shifting all about. She immediately went to Red and told her of the encounter, but when her lover looked out the window, the men were gone.

Late that night, they returned in greater numbers, now very drunk and loud, and the din awakened the two women from their sleep. Red shot out the door to face them; ready, inconceivably, for attack. In Spanish, she berated them angrily for the disturbance and told them to leave. They replied by asking for money. Furiously, Red refused; telling them that money was for work well done, not drunkenness and harassment, admonishing them to find work. No, they said, there was never work in the town. Red said they would get nothing here and ordered them to leave, then returned, red-faced and breathless, to bed. The last thing Jean saw was the gleam of the men's eyes, hatred and impotence congealing, in the glow of the flashlight. The two women listened uneasily and talked for a time, pondering this terrible end to their efforts. But they sensed it differently—a nausea and dull anxiety filled Jean; for Red, rage blotted out all else. Here was another thing to fight for, and without a thought, she jumped into the fray. Jean's anxiety increased as she sensed these changes, for she knew that Red, when angered, could not stop fighting. But Red was now much older, and her heart did not have its former strength. Now Red, too, held danger. The implications suddenly spread out before Jean like a huge, dark tree, full of unknown, resonant power.

It seemed impossible to sleep and yet, toward morning, they did so. Jean had a strange, recurrent dream. She knew she was asleep, dreaming, but her eyes were half-open, and she could see the room in darkness. The dark was filled with unknown, moving things. Swift fingers moved about, legs ran back and forth pointlessly, and nothing came into focus for the dark. There was a haunting sound: an ancient stringed instrument cried out softly in an unknown melody, each note so piercingly sweet and painful that she knew it would always exist, outside of time. It could never be diminished or forgotten. It partook of no dynamic process but simply was: dark, melodious, eloquent beyond words but not music, exquisite eyeless pain, horribly sweet, beautiful, ceaseless. Jean's consciousness seemed to float, and at last she saw the house from outside through fractured moonlight, the windows broken.

When she awoke, her stomach and entrails felt as though she had been on a moving ship all night, seasick. The two women talked for a long time, deciding that they must try to regain control of themselves and the situation and do what was necessary to find some satisfaction in their new life. Now Red began exhorting them toward self-control and action. Grimly but calmly, they spent the day in their usual pursuits—reading, writing, gardening. Slowly, they began to push back the dark. Towards evening, however, a silent fear began to possess them, and they found themselves strangely distracted and irritable. They took no pleasure in the sounds of nightfall, the rippling motion of water in the lake and the alternating, rhythmic cries of birds and insects. One creature, bird or insect, was suddenly dominant. It made a wailing cry that seemed to soar, brilliant and resonant, to a height; then plummet downward—low, tremulous and deep as a piano bass chord. Jean followed its exquisite, painful beauty helplessly, as she had the stringed instrument in her dream. Her breathing stopped each time she heard it. They did not look out the windows, which were carefully covered with drapes.

Toward midnight, as they were preparing for bed, a rock was hurled through the second story's wall of windows. Instantly, they knew they had been expecting this sound all day, perhaps from the beginning of the house's construction. Red grabbed a flashlight and ran outside, finding more than a half-dozen men drunk and laughing. When she began yelling at them, they said they could now offer their services to fix the window—for money, *señora mamacita*, for money. Red continued to shout that they would get no money for destroying property and ran furiously back inside the house, opening the desk drawers in search of the revolver. As her hand clutched it, another rock came crashing through the window. Red bellowed in rage like an animal and ran back outside, still crying out. She shot the revolver over the men's heads, the shots roared in the black sky, and the men ran off.

Then she came back inside and called the police. Jean only sat in a chair before her, stunned and frightened. Her eyes never left Red's face and she watched, in terror at her lover's rage and the havoc it could produce for her heart. "Calm down, honey," she said over and over again. "You can't get sick over this." But Red was possessed by her rage and would not listen.

Finally, she reached a police officer who took her complaint by telephone. When he heard their address, he suddenly became evasive, however, and said that it was a very busy night and no one could come immediately. "We're under a bloody siege," Red said in Spanish. The officer's tone altered artificially, and he said it was not, perhaps, such an emergency, *senora*. The men were obviously just having some fun. They were drunk. What did she expect from drunken men? Surely, her husband did the same. Red became even more enraged. She said thank god, she had no husband and accused the officer of passivity and making excuses for the men, infantilizing them. She added that even he himself was a child if he did not take responsibility for upholding the laws against reckless, willful destruction of property. This seemed to go straight over the officer's head and he merely repeated, again, that they were men and she, a woman, as though it was a law that superceded all others. Red shouted that someone had better come or she would speak to his supervisor and every district congressman or woman, at last slamming the phone down.

"I can't say I didn't expect it," she said in a slightly lower voice. "It's only our dysfunctional police, of course."

"And now it's happening to us," Jean said. "It's in our backyard."

"But, you'd think they could deal with a little thing like this. It has nothing to do with murdered women and great mysteries. It's only wanton destruction of property."

They waited. Nothing happened. And Red fumed still more. Passivity was far worse than action for her. Jean stared at her in abject terror. Red had never been enraged like this before, even prior to her treatment for blood pressure. Now Jean knew she could lose far more than the house. She could lose Red, everything. "How can you let this bother you so much," Jean said in fear. "You didn't get this enraged over the murders."

"That's because I could so something!" Red shouted again. "I could fight a war! I could save womens' lives. I can't do a damned thing about this!" Jean touched, caressed her lover, trying helplessly to calm her. But another spasm of rage convulsed Red, and she leaped up, pounding her fists senselessly on the walls. Jean felt terror so dark, so consuming that everything vanished and she sat still, gasping for breath, thinking of nothing but Red.

The police did not come until the following afternoon. Inspecting the broken windows, the officers smiled and shook their heads in bemused amazement at the drunken revel enjoyed by the men. Red's eyes and mouth were dark with wrath, and she demanded action that would protect them from further harassment. The officers again smiled, and one uttered a low whistle, as though they were being asked the impossible. Then they requested a donation to some sort of policemen's benevolent association, a bald request for a bribe. Red ordered them out of the house. "Money!" she shouted. "Goddamned money! Give it to thugs or thieves, your choice."

"It's just what all the women said. They're all completely corrupt. We have to deal with this ourselves, and we can."

Red snapped instantly back into action by calling the lawyer. Jean sat beside her, still terrified, listening to Red's responses. The lawyer, it seemed, asked a strange series of questions: Who did they know in the community? Anyone from across the bridge? Had they made any donations to the PRI Party? Did they have any relatives who were native Mexicans? Red's answers were all negative, then she asked, "Are you saying they don't enforce the laws if you're not living among the wealthy or have connections who do?" The lawyer suddenly became evasive and replied no, of course not, *senora*, but he ended the conversation by recommending that they make the requisite donation to the police as a last resort. His tone clearly implied, however, that they should do so immediately; it *was* their last resort. He reminded them that they were two women alone in the unpatroled area.

Again, Red slammed the phone down and looked for the first time at Jean. Jean instantly seized the initiative and told her that her blood pressure was much, much too high and that they must see a doctor immediately. Red agreed sarcastically, saying yes, the men would not be back until they were drunk again. Her voice was ragged, her eyes glittered as though feverish, and her sarcasm ran like a bull. Jean grabbed her arm and pulled her to the car. But at the last moment, Red shook herself loose and walked, insanely, back into the house. "No, I won't leave!" she said. "Not for a moment. It's ours, we worked for it, and they've never worked for anything but their damned booze! I'll shoot those bastards if I have to!" Jean stared at her in terror, hardly hearing her words. In agony, all she registered was that Red was refusing treatment and placing herself in greater danger. The implications were now as thick as a forest and she was lost. She could not think. She merely held Red, and the two women knew nothing but the other's breathing.

That evening after dark, another rock came crashing through the window. Red ran outside so fast that she forgot the flashlight. She did not shoot over their heads, but with slightly greater precision. In the dark, however, she was far away from her mark repeatedly. "Go away and never come back!" she roared in Spanish. "I'll kill every one of you." The men dispersed again. Then she lurched back inside with the gun and fell onto the sofa. "Well, this is the new Wild West," she said. "You need both a gun and a flashlight, and I forgot the damned flashlight."

"Thank god!" Jean cried. "Now you listen to me! Your blood pressure is much, much too high, and you're acting like a madwoman. You could have killed them and yourself—think of that! I won't have it! You come with me now to the emergency room of the hospital. Those men are gone but regardless of them, I won't lose you! I don't want a dead lover, and I don't want dead Indians. The last thing I care about is this damned glass house!"

"OK. OK," said Red, suddenly pliable in exhaustion. "You're right. I don't want to kill them, and I don't want to die over a herd of pigs." They both took a long breath and held each other, filled with a new purpose. Then they left immediately.

Their wait in the hospital was full of constant din, trucks roaring by outside like a fleet of jets, babies shrieking, five bawling, cursing men who had been knifed or shot, and even chickens and goats running insanely through the door as it opened. "Well, we should have gone to the one over the bridge, as usual," said Red. "Is this a hospital or a barnyard?"

"It's Mexico, my love," Jean said with a smile. "It's our new barnyard, Mexico." Red smiled helplessly, and Jean saw that her coloring was somewhat more normal. Then they noticed a baby pig that had wandered in. Carefully and delicately, it defecated in front of the roaring television.

"The only creature with some restraint in all of Mexico," Red commented. The two women screamed with laughter and horror as the smell reached them and rushed for paper towels from the bathroom to clean it up. No one else seemed to notice. "It's for Mexico, honey," Red said. "It's our donation to its benevolence."

They were fast asleep when Red was finally called by the doctor. A tiny, ancient, silver-haired Mexican, the only doctor on duty, told Red that her blood pressure was so high she would be dead in a matter of weeks or months if they could not, somehow, bring it down. He confessed that he was uncertain of how this could be done since she was already on medication. The most extreme measures, which must be done in a hospital, were inherently temporary and impractical. He finally decided that he would add another drug, a calcium channel blocker, as well as increasing the doses of her other blood pressure medications. At night, if the noise continued, she must also take a tranquilizer, a sleeping pill or both.

"Well that should make me a sweet little zombie, fast asleep in a half-destroyed house!" Red exclaimed. "When I'm completely demented, I'll come back here and hang out with the pigs." The doctor looked at her in bewilderment, and Red realized that she was too tired to speak Spanish. She had been speaking English.

When they left the hospital, they agreed that they wanted nothing but sleep. It was a good sign, Jean decided. She immediately began to argue that they must, after sleeping, return to the U.S. so that a more competent doctor could treat Red. Red agreed but first, she said, she wanted to be treated by a more competent policeman. She marched into the police station and asked to see the two officers who had visited them at the house. "I want to give them," she said carefully in Spanish, "a donation for the policemen's benevolent association." This produced an immediate response, and they were escorted politely to the two officers. They found them drinking beer, eating enchiladas, and listening to loud mariachi music. The air was thick with marijuana smoke. "I see it is another very busy time," said Red, pulling a wad of money out of her pocket and handing it to the officers. "For your benevolent association and more good times. Now, will you please be benevolent and stop those men from destroying our house?"

"Oh, *si, si, señora*," they responded, rising instantly to their feet and even removing their hats politely. "Your donation will help so much with the poor babies."

"I think I know just what kind of babes he means," Red said in English to Jean. "To the benevolence of your whorehouse, gentlemen." The officers handed her a card with another telephone number and told the two women to call immediately if the men returned. Jean and Red left. "We're better off paying the police than those assholes," Red concluded. "They've got firearms, and they'll shoot with such benevolence."

"Why don't those men have guns, too?" Jean asked.

"I don't know," said Red. "They may not have the money to buy them or opportunity to steal them. They probably have knives." Jean instantly made Red promise that she would return to the U.S. for treatment, that it was the only solution.

"There has to be some way of doing this so that no one gets killed," she concluded. They returned home and slept, deeply and dreamlessly, for many hours. The downstairs doorbell suddenly rang.

"They're not drunk yet, so it's not our assholes," Red said. "I'll answer it."

"Be careful anyway." Red put on her bathrobe and went downstairs. When she opened the door, Maria, Pepita, Blanca, Rosa and a throng of other women were outside.

"Excuse my appearance," Red said. "Our nights are rather active these days."

"That's why we've come," Maria said. "We've heard about what is happening, and we would be very poor friends indeed if we did not offer you shelter and support."

Red smiled and tried to look both pleased and casual. "This really isn't something from which we need to be saved: it's just a dispute with the workmen who built the house. Our lives are not threatened, and I want you to rest easily on that. This is a little spat we have to ride out."

Pepita came forward. "But remember, you've been noticed by the killers. You may not be as safe as you think."

"This is just something we have to go through, and I don't believe it's life-threatening. I can't imagine just giving them my house. It's as simple as that. This will be over when they understand they can't get any more money out of us. Until then, we stay. We'll have a party for you when it's all done."

Pepita reached forward and squeezed Red's hand. Her face had become tragic. "I have a very bad feeling about this. Please, be very careful. We have come to love the two of you." Tears appeared in her eyes.

"We will be very careful. Remember, we've got guns, and now we sleep with them right beside us. There is no need for so much concern. I would invite you all in, but as it stands, we sleep during the day and are awake all night. I must say goodnight to you all. We thank you and we love you, too." The women murmured their goodnights and good lucks and turned away, except Pepita, who looked back with doubt and tears in her eyes. Red went back to bed. "It was . . ." she began.

"I heard everything," Jean said. "They are all wonderful. I've come to love them, too."

"We've got to get more sleep." Red embraced Jean, and they fell asleep again. It was close to midnight when they were awakened by a sound: glass breaking on the second floor.

"'The Wild West,' episode two," said Red, now rising slowly. "I can feel that new drug. I think I'll stay calm." She did not go outside this time but rather, called the police on the new line, telling them in Spanish to come quietly without headlights and catch the men in front of the house. The police now came immediately and pounced on the men like animals in the dark. The men tried to run, but the police shot three of them and tackled two. Then they pistol-whipped them all into near-unconsciousness. The wounded men were simply manacled and dragged into the police van without medical attention. It seemed doubtful any would survive. Two of the men managed to escape, one by jumping into the lake and powerfully swimming underwater. As the last men were dragged away, the two women saw agony and terror on their faces. The sight was horribly shocking. They had never expected such brutality from the police, which they immediately recognized as more criminal than anything the men had done. As the police drove off with their bloody plunder like hunters carrying animal carcasses, the two women sat, stunned and speechless, in the house, which was securely locked.

"I don't want to see anything like that again as long as I live," Jean said at last. "Don't ever call the police." Red replied by tearing the card to shreds.

"I had no idea they would do that . . ." Red felt nothing but shock and compassion. "I'm so sorry, honey."

"What have we done?" asked Jean sadly.

"What can't money buy here? I actually paid to have them tortured and killed."

"How can this be happening? How can they do that?"

"The men are from the wrong side of the bridge. Apparently, that's how and why," said Red in exhaustion.

"Oh my god," said Jean in wonder. "And we actually chose to live here. I want out! I just want out of here."

"Not tonight, honey," said Red. "Let's just get some sleep. We need it."

"God, we need it! I could lose consciousness forever and not care a bit."

They lay in bed in the dark, holding each other, stroking, kissing, trying to find the center again, the love, intimacy, trust, that was nowhere. How utterly foolish they were, they thought, and perhaps said it. They took off their clothing and continued touching, holding, throwing back, again, the dark. Then they made love uncontrollably as they had when they were young, explosively, with the violence of love when all is lost. Again and again, Jean found her legs over Red's shoulders, having orgasms. Until the morning light, they coupled: they could not stop. The fear and anger, the frustration, were all released; for here, now, Jean could trust Red again. She could trust her to live, to give and take pleasure, in spite of all they had lost in this brutal, impossible place, there was the love, always that, the feel and surface of the body, naked, the skin purely, to be touched and caressed and to respond, an explosion of love uncontained until the dark, the unconsciousness, though it became day. They were unconscious, sleeping, lovers, that forever, if nothing else, lovers.

They slept deeply, lovingly, in the bright sunlight and awoke again at night, their life cycles now reversed. Immediately, they kissed and smiled, felt relaxed. "I think my blood pressure went down," Red said.

"That's good to hear," Jean said. They touched each other's faces in silence and thought that the tumult was, perhaps, at bay. They had blotted it out with love. The door bell rang again.

"Once again, it can't be our nightly assholes. It must be the women again. I'll answer it, " Red said.

"I'm coming with you." They put on their bathrobes and went downstairs. When they opened the door, Clara, Teresa and Nieves stood before them, each one with a giant kitchen knife.

"We are here to fight and die with you," Clara said. "We've heard it all."

Red and Jean carefully resisted the desire to laugh, and Jean said, "There is no danger of death or anything else here. It's just a spat between us and the men who built the house. We don't need warriors, though we do understand that you are very strong and fierce."

"Oh, yes," Red said.

"We've heard otherwise," Teresa said. "They told us everything, the women who were murdered, everything."

"We want to fight them and die if we must," Nieves said. "They took my sister, and I must kill them with you." She had a wild, determined look on her face that was reflected on the other girls' faces.

Red and Jean looked at one another, then Red nodded that she would try to handle it. "It's true. You're right, but they are very, very strong and fierce. We will all die, so you must return one last time to your mothers and tell them what you need on your *ofrendas*, which they will build after your deaths. They must know that, so your souls will always be able to come back on the Day of the Dead."

"You must go back one last time," Jean agreed. "Think of their hopeless grief if they could not see you again every year."

"That's right," Clara said, her face suddenly thoughtful.

"But they won't let us come back if they know," Teresa said. "Red and Jean are trying to trick us."

"We would never lie about a matter of life and death," Jean added.

"That's true, too," Nieves said.

"When they try to restrain us, we'll just all run out of the house," Clara said. "We already know that they can't keep up."

"Yes," said Teresa. "They can't."

"OK," Nieves said. "We'll be right back. Leave the door open."

"We will," Red said, "and we welcome you as great warriors." The three girls ran off into the night. Red immediately locked the door. "Their mothers will have them under lock and key as soon as they hear of it, thank god. We'll never see them again until this is over."

"But it was a close call, and I must say, I have a brilliant lover."

"You get flexible when you have so many problems." They laughed all the way back upstairs and then slept together in the dark until they heard the inevitable sound of windows breaking on the second story.

"Oh, my god," said Red. "They saw what happened to their cronies, and they came back for more. I don't believe it!"

"Get the gun and the flashlight," Jean said. "It could be worse now." Without turning on the lights, they found the gun and the flashlight. They were still naked and didn't even think of clothes. Looking outside, they saw that two men stood boldly in front of the house. Jean saw that strange look again in their eyes, as though it lived there and nothing else existed. Even in the dark, it was there, fluid, fluent, changing. It was part of the dark. It was the dark.

Red shot the gun over their heads again but aimed closer. The men twitched at the roar, then just stood there, dark, panting, awful with that intoxicated, lost energy in their glittering eyes. "They have no idea what they're doing," Jean said. "They're just waiting to be killed."

"Turkeys waiting to be headless on Thanksgiving," said Red. "'The Wild West,' episode three. We're the lesbians, they're the Indians. Let's shoot."

"Now just you wait a minute! We have other choices here. We don't have to play this game," Jean said. "We don't have to kill Indians. They're not the murderers; they're impoverished men who can't find work. We can just leave. You need to go to the U.S. anyway."

"I won't give up, dammit!" Red said. "I won't just sit back and let them take what's mine."

"You won't? Even when it makes you kill Indians, when it leaves you dead of a heart attack? You still won't leave?"

"No, I won't give it up. I'm just not a little girl who lets the big bad man take my house away from me! Dammit, I won't! And besides, the war could start again with those killers. It's just waiting to happen. We haven't even talked about that. Who will shelter the women?"

"Oh god," said Jean. "I don't think I can leave you alone here with them. If you won't leave, I can't. Oh god . . ." she nearly sobbed.

"Welcome to 'The Wild West.' Take your gun."

"Why?" Jean asked, terrified.

"I might not always be here. You need target practice. Shoot."

"I won't kill an Indian! I'll stay with you but by god, I won't kill."

"So just aim a little closer, then miss. That's what I've been doing." Jean took the gun uncertainly and tried to aim it close to one man's ear. It would roar deafeningly. Maybe he'd finally run. She fired; the gun roared. The man just twitched and stood still like an animal to be slaughtered, panting and sweating, impossible.

"Don't you see?" Jean said. "They don't even want to live. It doesn't matter whether we shoot them or not. They'll just be there, eyes in a slaughterhouse."

"Look. Here's what we know. One, we're not calling the police. Two, they don't care whether they live or die. So, threaten them with a fate worse than death. Aim closer to the testicles. That should be good for something. They can't lose those *cajones*."

"I don't believe this is happening. I must still be asleep. I know perfectly well that I didn't come to Mexico to shoot Indians. In the ear or the testicles."

"Now we deal with what *is*. Of course, we didn't come here for that, but that's what we found. Do you want those police back here? You'll puke your guts out. You. Shoot now. You do it."

"Oh god," Jean said and aimed to miss. The bullet landed in the ground between one man's legs. The two men suddenly clenched up in terror like cloth puppets and ran. Jean and Red lay on the floor in the darkness in silence.

"It worked," said Jean.

"You bet it did."

"But now we've escalated. And now they know we don't want to kill them, and we won't call the police. That will make them escalate, too. Just what do you think you're going to do about that?"

And then they talked, talked wearily, endlessly, and a bit insanely for hours, just lying on the floor in the dark. Over and over, they asked the same questions: why can't we leave? Why not? Who will shelter the women if we give up? Is it better to kill Indians, men who haven't murdered anyone? But we won't kill them! We'll just hold out longer. But will it work? And what about the consequences of its not working? Everyone wants to survive: you just push the right buttons. Leave now! Just leave for godssake! I'm not leaving this place to that slime! But why us? We were good to them. They've forgotten already. But why, why us, why anyone? Because we have money. Because we're foreigners. Because we don't like killing people. Because we can't shoot worth a shit. Because.

And below, beneath, it came again and again to Jean. Because we're women and they're men. Women who won't do what they want. Because we're lesbians. Because it's me. Because I've never wanted a man enough to take him joyously, tenderly between my legs the way I take Red, the way she takes me. And I already want her. I want her to blot it out now and make love to me. Love me. Now.

Jean touched Red again softly, tenderly. The two women said nothing and caressed one another in the dark. Again, they made love uncontrollably and pushed back the dark. Until it would come again. What was it now but flesh, skin, joy, and then the dark, the men, a gun, roaring? "Let's just sleep now," Jean whispered, "until it starts again." For surely, surely, it would start again. Sleep in the light, warm with love, shoot in the dark, chaotic, senseless, inevitable, now unconscious, asleep.

They awoke in bed, still naked in each other's arms, their guns lying on each side of the bed, the flashlight on the other. They looked at each other and knew they had slept deeply and well. "It's starting to agree with you," said Red. "You look wonderful."

"No, it doesn't agree. I've just given up. I can't get you out of here, and I can't leave you alone here."

"You shouldn't. The sex is just too good to leave."

"That's the odd part. I haven't figured that out yet. We should be half dead with anxiety."

"You're lowering my blood pressure. I thank your goddess-like sexual power for restoring my health."

"Let's eat," said Jean. Without turning on the lights, for it was dark now, they ate and drank, touched and talked. Again, they never thought of putting clothes on but walked about, naked. What was it now but sleep, sex and shooting? They didn't even bother to observe that everyone had gone crazy, themselves included. It was too obvious.

"Well, are we so perverse that we will call the police?" asked Red.

"No, no," said Jean. "We'd have to be foaming at the mouth. We're quieter madwomen than that."

"Except when we shoot the gun, of course,"

"Excepting that."

"Let me say," said Red, "that I've never enjoyed our endlessly orgasmic bodies more in my life. I think I love you like a bull."

"Good. You've been acting like a bull since this thing started. I like the tender, sexy bull better than the mad one with the high blood pressure. You can break into my china shop anytime.

You're gorgeous. You're unearthly. I've never wanted you this much."

"You're the St. Teresa of orgasms."

"You, too."

"Two of them! Two roman candles going off in the center of Mexico!" They laughed uproariously. "Is this what we came to Mexico for?"

"Don't even try, my love, to make sense of this. It will never make sense. We were librarians for thirty years. We did not come to Mexico to lead a revolution, shoot Indians, have spectacular sex and stop wearing clothes."

"Apparently, we had no idea what we were doing."

Silently, they went to the second story, gun and flashlight in hand, to assess the damage. Nearly the entire wall lay in shards about its wooden frame. Cold, hard, glittering pieces of glass flashed fiercely over the floor. There was nothing left for the men to destroy. "This looks like a vomit of diamonds from a dragon's maw," said Red.

"Is that what it looks like? It's our dream in a million pieces. What are they going to come up with next? Do you think they'll bring fire to burn us out? Fire's cheap enough."

"Then we walk out shooting, and they don't get the house."

"Then what's next?"

"I don't know. I just know it's happening with the most wonderful woman in the world." They kissed hungrily, their bodies pressed together.

"We shouldn't get started yet," Jean said, breathless. "We can't shoot and make love at the same time."

"Oh, I don't know about that. With discipline, we could."

"They'll be here any moment. Let's get out of the ruins." They walked back downstairs and lay on the floor in the dark. Some indefinable time later, a huge crashing roar boomed straight through the door. The two women looked at the door in shock.

"They've got an ax," Red roared. "They're coming through!" She held the gun firmly and pointed straight for the door. The two women now crouched behind the living room couch. They did not shine the flashlight. Not yet. They waited.

"If they come through, I'll kill them," said Red. "I have to now. I'm so sorry, baby." Jean waited, stiff with horror, clenching Red's arm with her hand. Even in the dark, she could see that Red's rage had returned in full force. Her face and lips were nearly black in the dark. I should have made her go back with me to the States, Jean thought. I should have been stronger. I should have resisted her. I should never have let it go this far. We could have gotten away with our lives and not killed anyone. Jean didn't even look at the door. She watched Red's face in terror. The whole world was a door crashing, bursting open under the force of an ax.

But, incredibly, Red relaxed and leaned back on the floor, the gun falling to her side. In horror, Jean saw that she was not breathing, and her face was ashen in the dim light. No, no! she thought. She tried to give her air, mouth-to-mouth, all the while the door, the door! Now she could hear it cracking, bursting, falling to pieces, done, finished, and so was Red. Without a thought, she aimed her gun.

Two massive, dark men grunted, stumbled into the doorway, covered with dust and dirt, stinking like animals. The smell of alcohol and sweat was instantly all over the room as they lurched blindly, stupidly into the space, the sacred space they had been denied and now conquered with their brutality, stupidity, reeking their musk. They both sweated profusely and seemed insane, demented, ooze pouring off their bodies and faces. Out of the dark . . . her thoughts no longer completed themselves. They were wearing masks Jean had seen before, and she recognized their bodies: the big, clumsy man and the smaller, more muscular man whose body had the perfection of a dancer. Jean thought, it's them, the killers. They're here, in front of me.

One carried a knife, one an ax. From the floor, they looked like immense, raging black bulls that had come, dripping, from Hell, their minds and hearts dissolved in fire. The stocky man whispered, "*Mamasotos*, where are you? We know you are here. We will find you." His voice was a whispering sing-song, softly wheedling its awful words. Lurching, stumbling, a nightmare, they came. "We have come to give you pleasure, *mamasotos* and take your souls. Beautiful, beautiful *mamasotos*," the big man whispered sing-song.

"Shut up!" the smaller man said; though he seemed every bit as demented. They were so drugged that they could barely stand or walk. They stumbled; they blundered; yet, the smaller, more muscular man looked quite dexterous with his knife. He whipped it around himself lovingly as though it were alive, a graceful, gentle motion.

"And I will turn you into *mamacitas*, red ones, all bloody, lovely to the touch; and I will touch you harshly, all I want to, *mamacitas*."

Jean aimed her gun carefully, yet a flood of thought, of agony, of horror stopped her. At once: Red was dead, and all was lost. What did anything matter? "*Mamasotos, mamacitas*," whispered the big man in his singsong, insane.

Then a memory, a fierce one, full of love and rage, filled Jean. She felt, again, that strong, firm hand cover hers as it had so long ago on a golden California afternoon, pull the trigger, blaze a hole in the dark, turn a man into a corpse. The big man screamed, dropped the ax, then picked it up again with greater control and raised it to strike. Jean fired again, and he fell, unmoving, to the floor.

Jean moved to Red and again touched her face. It was already cold, for Red had died when the gun fell out of her hand. "My darling, my love," she whispered with unspeakable tenderness, then rose to look at the dead mens' faces beneath their masks. Carlos' mouth was open in surprise, his eyes utterly blank. For a moment, she envied him. Now he was blank, unfeeling, gray, gone from this awful world. Diego's face looked hideous, his eyes bulging with terror and fury, his mouth a hole. She averted her eyes immediately.

She returned to her lover and caressed her again and again; kissed her cheeks, throat, hands, thighs, at last held her in her arms, wordless, and fell into the dark herself. There was a sound, a low moaning, constantly uttered over them, and later she recognized that it came from her own throat.

Now they were all dead, all gone. It was over. It's over, my darling. Now you can stay here. You're free, she thought, insanely. The killers are dead now. It's over. Such thoughts she had, over and over, until first light broke upon her. Her eyes opened upon that endless garden of beauty. Different insects now, different birds uttered rhythmic cries, always a swelling rush of sound. She listened for the wailing one she had heard before. It was everywhere at once, wailing, wailing the notes one must helplessly follow, so sweet, exquisite, so painful, ceaseless.

The soft light streaked gently, horribly, oozing blood spilling outward, wordless and inevitable, across the room. The room held the horrible light. It could not refuse. She looked up and knew she was back in the old, small, unspeakably terrible world. She was alive, a living horror. The only one left. The one who fired the gun. If she could, she would push back the day, the light, and be a creature of the dark, dripping and stinking the blackness, like the men who had axed through the door.

She walked, naked, the gun in her hand, outside and looked at the lake. What a senseless, foolish, insane profusion of beauty it was. The wind stirred over her naked skin and blew her hair. And now they, the beautiful things, were all beginning again in their innocence, their insanity. How awful was this light and how awful, too, the beauty it illuminated. So little sense, justice, compassion, did it have. It did not strive to be better. It just was: beautiful, haunting, touching the multitudes of her being as though she were a stringed instrument. The world was just a young creature, thoughtlessly moving its gorgeous limbs, rushing, galloping, becoming the soft, gentle Mexican light that had utterly deluded them all. Beneath it, she was alone, destroyed, naked with a gun.

Then an unspoken purpose stirred within her. Not knowing why, she bent over Red and placed the gun in her hand, bending her fingers carefully around the trigger, then let the gun rest over her stomach. It was what Red would have wanted. With her dying breath, she had wanted to kill the murderers and save the women and girls from them forever, but she had died seconds before she could do it. Again, the low, moaning sound escaped her, and she held her lover to her breast and kissed her one last time. Red was ice-cold, already becoming someone else. This meant she could leave. The spell was broken.

Then it all began moving much faster, whatever it was. A clock was now ticking, ticking in her head, however it happened. She dressed, packed a few things and got into the car. Helplessly, she turned for one moment to look back at the house with its demolished second story and, yet, its soaring, majestic beauty. Its immense, foolish, senseless, majestic beauty beneath the inevitable light. How riotous, burgeoning, alive and mad that beauty was. The house rearing up, majestic and terrible, was now a tomb, a headstone, to the grave holding her lover's body and that of the men who had desired nothing more than the pleasure of killing women and girls.

The engine fired, and she drove for the border. By early afternoon, she was there, smiling and waving her American passport, passing effortlessly over the border and back in the States, not that much better, after all, than Mexico; for where are women safe from men? Yet, it was farther, oh yes, much farther away from that hauntingly beautiful house where her lover's life had ended, and she had killed two men.

Then it went still faster. She took a cheap motel room in Southern California, lay on the edge of a flimsy, pink bed, and lost consciousness for sixteen hours. She woke in a frenzy of hunger and thirst, saw the hazy-gray light of Southern California and its blank-buzzing, crisscrossing, game-like terrain; artificially imposed on no more than a desert. It was every bit as ugly and tawdry as it looked: this judgement gave her satisfaction. Then slaking her thirst and hunger in a diner, just a glimmer of thought broke through. She went to the nearest bank and transferred all of her money out of Mexico and into her accounts in the US. I will give the house to the women in the village, she thought. They can use it as a home for battered women . . . Again she was pulled by the vast, thoughtless urge to move and was back on the road north, full of ocean, palms, sand and more light reflecting on waves to the point of a knife, until a dark fog invaded the road. It was night in Big Sur. Snaky-white fingers of fog beckoned her over the cliffs, and the only thing that stopped her was the thought of all those women and girls she loved. They would be safe now. They would live their lives and be stronger. She pulled away from the cliff and drove on and on.

Until she came through my doorway, hardly looking about her, not even seeing the dog, cat, snake, rat, fish and lizard, though they all eyed her. She came to me, to the room that was taken for granted, for it completed the symmetry; the space of healing and gentleness that had to be there. Then slowly, slowly, the feelings poured out, the tales we tell one another, those coarse, rough things came forth; crushed and wounded, halting, stumbling, understood in a flood, then incomprehensibly strange, eerie, bizarre and brutal. It was a story like that.

Now, she's sleeping in the extra room. The room is simple, just a bed, a chest of drawers, not much on the walls, no memories abounding, a place no dream ever made. I judged it sufficient for her to recover, with luck. I was there, in my small wooden house in San Francisco behind the overgrown garden. I'm no dreamer, and I don't travel for long periods. I'll always be here, as long as I breathe and write poetry, to keep the room open. She'll be here for some time. In the morning light, she'll be able to consider things like how to get Red's body out of Mexico, what she'll tell the Mexican police, and how to give the house to the Mexican women. Now, in the darkest night we ever know, she cannot. She can only sleep and fight for her sanity. Luck is with us, though. She made it out of there and all the way here, the longest distance she'd ever crossed in all her worldly travels. Yes, it was enough, that elusive quantity without which, we'd have nothing but beauty and dark.

# Afterword & Bibliography

However bizarre, violent, improbable and perverse the events of this novel may seem at times, the truth of the murders of women in Ciudad Juarez is orders of magnitude more so. The number of murders has been tallied as at least 370 according to the Mexican police and into the thousands according to investigative journalists covering the story. As in my novel, the murders have been carried out over many years and reveal total carelessness and failure on the part of the police. As in my story, there is evidence of devil worship in carved images left on the bodies as well as rumors of a wealthy family's involvement. The murders are still being carried out today, and the Mexican police still ignore them.

The novel's location is an impoverished section of Monterrey, Mexico that a friend of mine and I visited in the 1970s. We picked out Monterrey for a vacation by placing a blind finger on a map of Mexico and were astonished to find that it was indeed filled with PRI luxury homes and what seemed to be another small village just beyond a rickety wooden bridge. I have since made many trips to various parts of Mexico and have used my memory for description and scenes.

Some things mentioned in the novel are of course debatable. For example, there is a concept of an afterlife in ancient Indian religions, though my description of "three deaths" that end within human memory is more common, or so I speculate. Similarly, there are several hundred ancient gods in Mexican Indian mythology. I took a few basic nature gods and imagined them as a madman might envision them. My work is fiction and not fact with which an historian would agree. One could also debate the extent of womens' participation in the sacred dances in Mexican villages, whether identical twins ever share thoughts, and several other events of the novel.

I also read a number of books. The ones I ultimately found most helpful took as their subjects the Day of the Dead, Mexican celebrations, Mexican folklore and Mexican masks worn in dances on fiesta days in rural areas of Mexico and also in impoverished areas on the edges of some big cities. I was delighted to discover and use a wonderful collection of stories for children, *Fiesta Femenina*, about strong women, both natural and supernatural, in Mexican folklore; this was the basis for Pepita's bedtime stories for the children who stayed in Red and Jean's house. Every one of Pepita's stories is based on an actual legend from one of the many regions and tribes of Mexico. These books are listed below. I read many more books for background without using any of their information. I am a great admirer of D.H. Lawrence's novels but was surprised by the frequent racism of his travelogue, *Mornings in Mexico*. It was abundantly clear at least to me that the constantly referenced "savage" hostility he found in the Zapotecs and Hopi Indians was an effect of their sensing his racism.

Of course, I used the Internet to find very specific information on climate, flora and fauna in the area and to resolve several other questions that came to me as I wrote.

Poet and lesbian feminist Lynne Lonidier, the narrator of the story, was my friend in San Francisco many years ago. She did live in a small wooden house in the Mission district with a guest room for friends and women who found themselves suddenly in disturbing situations. She loved her pet dog and cat, and regularly kept a fish, lizard and snake, since she taught in the

San Francisco public schools and secretly liberated the biology labs of the animals that would otherwise be killed and dissected. She always kept a few at home and then placed them back into the closest approximation she could find of their natural habitat. She was very interested in the Indian perspective and made many trips to Mexico and South America to see it first-hand. I was always saddened by her early death and decided that I wanted her as my narrator, still alive, writing and doing what she loved to do. She was what we call, simply, good company—in life and hopefully in my novel as well. But, she is also a literary character and I make no claim of having rendered her with complete accuracy.

Eliot Porter and Ellen Auerbach, *Mexican Celebrations*, University of New Mexico Press, 1990.

Barbara Maudlin and Ruth D. Lechuga, *Masks of Mexico: Tigers, Devils and the Dance of Life,* Museum of New Mexico Press, 1990.

Kerry Arquette, Andrea Zocchi & Jerry Vigil, *Day of the Dead Crafts*, Wiley, 2008.

Mary-Joan Gerson & Maya Christina Gonzalez, *Fiesta Femenina: Celebrating Women in Mexican Folktale*, Barefoot Books, 2001.

Bev Jafek has published forty-five short stories and novel excerpts in the literary quarterly and university press publications. Some have been translated into German, Italian and Dutch and won many literary awards, including publication in the annual "prize" anthology, *The Best American Short Stories*. She was a Wallace E. Stegner Fellow in Fiction at Stanford and also won the Carlos Fuentes Award and the Editor's Prize for fiction from *Columbia: A Magazine of Poetry & Prose* as well as first prize in the Arch & Bruce Brown Foundation annual competition for "redemption of gay history" through creative writing. Her first story collection, *The Man Who Took a Bite Out of His Wife*, was published by Overlook Press (Penguin-Putnam). It was cited as one of the best story collections of the year in *The Year's Best Fantasy* (7th edition, Teri Windling) as well as being selected as a finalist for the Crawford Award (best new fantasy fiction writer of the year). Bev's first novel, *The Sacred Beasts*, was published by Bedazzled Ink in 2016, and her second story collection, *Three Nights of Love: International Stories, Tales & Creatures*, will be published by GusGus Books in July 2018